MOIRA

A young woman's journey through grief, trauma and growth

Helen Oxenham

Published by Inspiring Leadership International Limited.

First edition printed and published in the United Kingdom 2026.

A CIP catalogue record of this book is available from the British Library.

Any references to historical events, real people, or real places are used fictitiously. Names, characters, and places are products of the author's imagination.

ISBN (Paperback): 978-1-9191712-2-7
Imprint: Inspiring Leadership International Limited
Cover design: Fiona Myles
Editor: Fiona Myles
Typesetting: Matthew J Bird

Inspiring Leadership Foundation is a registered charity
in England and Wales (no 1165616).
Email: leigh@inspiringleadership-int.com
Website: https://inspiringleadership.foundation

Dedication

This book is dedicated to every adopted person.
We wander through life wondering 'what if'.
Our true identity is compromised.
We have a form of trauma unique to us.
Some overcome it and move on successfully, some simply don't.
Broken relationships, addictions, impulsive behaviour and a
myriad of other symptoms can overwhelm us.

And to Helen Oxenham who was never given the opportunity to
exist, but of course she is in me somewhere. To see her name on
the front of the book makes me feel like I have given Helen a
chance to be someone.
I am grateful I got to meet my biological families.
To be able to pull characteristics from both sides has filled in so
many holes in my heart.
Will I as an adoptee ever be whole? I don't know.
I am happy and at peace with who I am today.
Fiona Myles.

FOREWORD

There are moments when a story becomes far more than words on a page - it becomes a catalyst for change. *Write to Inspire* was created with a clear and heartfelt purpose: to elevate the voices of women through the power of literature. Through our *Write to Inspire* programme, we help women discover and develop their voice, supporting them from concept to publication - and strengthening their confidence as authors and change-makers. Every book we publish, across genres and journeys, contributes to this shared mission - nurturing creativity, compassion, and courage in the process.

The Inspiring Leadership Foundation is a charity dedicated to mobilising purpose-driven leaders and businesses to empower women. young people, and underserved communities helping them to dream big and achieve their full potential. Each *Write to Inspire* author is part of a growing collective united by purpose. Together, we commit a minimum of 10% of profits from every book to elevate the charity and the collective, directly supporting education, training, and career opportunities for underserved communities. This way, every page turned helps another voice rise.

Fiona's story (Fiona writes as Helen Oxenham) embodies exactly what *Write to Inspire* was created for - a celebration of lived experience, growth, and tenacity. Her words invite reflection, courage, and hope. It is a privilege to launch this book as part of the *Write to Inspire* movement and to see her voice join a powerful chorus of women changing the narrative for generations to come.

With gratitude,

Leigh Bowman-Perks
Founder, CEO, Inspiring Leadership Foundation

MOIRA

*A young woman's journey through
grief, trauma and growth*

ONE

IN THE BEGINNING

It was a bitterly cold night in the Scottish lowlands. Moira struggled to catch her breath as she lay in the woods with her baby about to enter the world. Afraid to cry out, even though she was sure no one would hear her up here. Biting her lip as yet another wave of excruciating pain caused her to want to scream.

No one knew she was here in the woods, in agony and alone, facing childbirth at fifteen years old. A quiet, studious girl who loved school, horses and adventures. This was one adventure she hadn't bargained on when she went out with Douglas Semple nine months ago! She prayed as waves of pain threw themselves up and over her body as her baby began its journey into the world.

Eventually, it was over. The baby was here. She cried as she managed the cord and waited for the next wave of afterbirth to come. She had spent hours in the library reading about pregnancy to help her manage what was to come. She was prepared for the next step. She was glad there had been none of the complications that had scared her half to death in the books she had read.

Trying hard not to look directly into her baby's eyes was so difficult. More than anything in that moment, she longed to tell her mum that she was pregnant. Her mother and father had lived in this tiny community all of their lives, as had her mother's family. How had she got into this predicament? Her parents were devout Christians. She knew they would have disowned her if they had ever found out she was pregnant, never mind having sex so young and unmarried. It was June 1966. You didn't have a baby at fifteen and expect to keep it and live happily ever after. Moira knew her mother would have sent her away to a home for pregnant girls, where she would have been told how bad she was and that she would give her baby up to strangers. A plan had formulated in her mind.

She had brought a change of clothes for herself and a blanket for the baby. She planned to take the baby to the Barnes Farmhouse on Bridge Lane. She knew that Fiona Barnes, who lived there, had been longing for a child for as long as Moira could remember. Moira had heard her talking about it week after week at church, while she sat and waited for her mum to finish serving the teas. She hated this part of her week. She was never allowed to help serve the drinks.

Moira's mother, Joy, was a bitter woman, always snapping and lashing out at home, sarcastically putting down Moira and anyone else who irritated her. Then she would slap on her Sunday smile when necessary. It pained Moira, especially as she got older. Why was her mum like this? Joy was like two different people. She never seemed happy, especially at home. She was glad she had her dad. He made her laugh. Making faces behind her mum's back when she started on her.

Moira felt a deep sadness as she wrapped her baby in the blanket, wishing she had a lovely, kind mum like her best friend Sally. Sally's mum would have kept the baby and helped Sally manage; she was sure of that. Trying not to look at her daughter was hard; she was crying as she bundled the baby up into her arms. She cried tears of real remorse for finding herself in this awful position. Moira tried to get herself together as the baby had started to cry now. Comforting her was hard, knowing what she had to do. It was a cold night, the baby felt cold, and she was feeling cold. Knowing she needed to do what had to be done quickly, before they both either got caught or died in the woods.

Settling the baby, she stole a glance at her, at those sweet little almond-shaped blue eyes. She looked away; she couldn't afford to connect with her. She wondered what Mrs Barnes would call her? Her heart skipped a beat for a second as she thought, *"What if Mrs Barnes didn't keep her?"* Panic began to set in; fear gripped her chest. A natural concern for the welfare of her child was setting in. She had no choice but to go to the farmhouse step as quickly as she could.

Moira knew the woods like the back of her hand. She had played here all through her childhood, walked the paths with her father and her friends. Moira quickly navigated her way to the edge of the woods where the Barnes property began. She made her way over the field as stealthily as she could. Her young body was wracked with pain. Her heart was hammering in her chest, cold sweat was trickling down her back. Being caught was not an option.

Hesitating as she looked at her baby, was she doing the right thing? Maybe she could take her home? Knowing that was not an option, she allowed the tears to flow down her face into the blanket.

The early morning noises seemed so loud in her head. Birds and small animals were doing their thing. Normally, those sounds would have delighted her, but right now, she wanted them to be quiet. Approaching the Barnes farm, she could smell the ducks and the chickens. The smell was making her feel sick. The emotional and physical pain she was in was making her feel sick, too.

Wrapped in her little grey blanket the baby was fairly quiet and beginning to warm from the heat of Moira's body; she just gave the odd whimper. She knew the moment she put the baby on the step, at the back door she would need to pray that a fox or another animal didn't kill her. Lights were on in the Barnes kitchen at 4.30 am. She knew they only had one dog, and it lived inside. It wasn't a working dog, they only kept poultry. Her heart was now hammering so hard she thought she would pass out. The fear of being caught, the worry about the baby being killed. The shame of what had just happened was all crashing in on her.

Put the baby down, Moira, put the baby down. She didn't want to, but with no choice, she laid the baby on the step as close to the door as she could and ran. She kicked their metal bucket as she dashed out of the courtyard, hoping it would bring Mrs Barnes to the door.

The fear that was hurtling around her chest was choking the breath from her young body, which was already completely exhausted and wracked with pain. She drew near to home with a heavy heart. She hadn't had to run far. All this trauma in the space of a few hours. Months' worth of fear and hiding the bump, thankfully, Moira had always been a bit on the plump side. There was still a bump, but no baby. It was safe, well, she hoped her daughter was safe in a lovely warm kitchen, and not being carried off to be some wild animal's meal; that thought almost caused her to throw up. She took a few minutes to regain some composure; her body was trembling, her heart was still pounding, and there was an awful fear nestling in the pit of her stomach. Moira walked slowly to her back door.

Back in her room, she lay on her bed for a moment and thought about the events of the night she had just endured. Why had she been so stupid, so weak? Never again. She knew she needed a bath before she went to school; it wasn't the norm to bathe in the morning, but she could say she had started her period. Something else she had had to lie about all this time, and she had a stack of sanitary towels under her bed, unused. The warm bath was not as comforting as she had thought it would be. She was still losing blood and in a lot of pain. Every time her mind thought of her baby, her heart leapt. As daylight fully emerged, she wondered if she should give the baby a name just for herself to think about as time went on. She asked herself whether that would make everything that had happened even more painful?

Hot tears ran down her face in the bath as the full realisation of what she had just done hit her. Emotionally drained, physically wrecked, she gave her baby a name. She named her child Helen.

Exhaustion was creeping in as the day wore on. Thankfully, it was a Friday. She could not concentrate at school at all; her mind was filled with thoughts of Helen and what was happening with her. Had they found her? Was she ok? Did an animal get her? Her heart lurched at that thought, and she gave a little gasp.

Mrs Caldwell looked up and saw Moira Kirkwell, white as a ghost.

"Moira, are you feeling unwell?"

Moira seized the chance to be sent home and told Mrs Caldwell she was most definitely going to be sick, and could she make her way home for the rest of the day?

After making her way to the secretary's office to get a pink slip to be signed by one of her parents, she could then let her mum know she had been sent home unwell. This would allow her to go home and get the rest her body and mind were craving. She was in a state of shock and exhaustion. Neither of her parents were home when she got in, so Moira had another warm bath and went to bed. Saving the sanitary towels had been a good idea; she was going through them fast.

Moira had left the pink slip on the table before she went upstairs, so her parents would know she was home. She woke up to her mum shouting at her to come and get her dinner. Moira no more wanted to go downstairs than she wanted to learn how to fly, but she knew everything had to appear relatively normal. Trying to eat her dinner was difficult. Moira knew she needed to eat, but her stomach was heaving.

Her mum, Joy, as usual, had a face that would curdle milk. Neither of her parents ever seemed to be happy. Her mum made everyone else feel unhappy by constantly seeing the worst in everyone and everything. Her dad was quietly unhappy. Coming home from work, sitting reading his paper or going to the local bar.

"I saw your pink slip, Moira. What is it that's wrong with you?"

Inside, she wanted to scream at her. I had a baby girl. Instead, she told her mum she had been sick that morning and felt unwell again at school; she felt the immediate fire of telling lies. It had been drummed into her all of her life that no liar would enter heaven's gates. Her mum often quoted a myriad of biblical threats for all occasions of bad behaviour.

Although her dad went to church with them and read his Bible in the morning, he didn't quote any fire and brimstone at her. She adored her dad. He would often take her out on light nights up into the woods after tea. On winter nights, he would read or play board games with her before he went to the pub. On weekends, they would make dens or go down to the river and float sticks, paddling or swimming together. It was always great fun with her dad. He told her often how much he loved her. She looked over at him, with his head in the paper. He was a handsome man, tall with jet black hair, and suntanned skin from working outside at the stables.

She had heard her mum berating almost everyone in the village at one time or another. No one pleased her mum; everyone always had their negative traits dragged across the table. Moira really hated hearing her mum going on about other people. Today of all days. Moira tried to imagine what her mum would have to say about someone else's daughter who had had a baby in the woods. The thought of it made her feel even worse than she already felt.

As she started to clear the table, Joy began to talk. "Bobby, have you heard the latest about the Barnes family? She has only gone and had a baby, a little girl, would you believe it? They told not a soul she was pregnant in case she had another loss. How many years has that been coming?"

Instead of being happy for her, Joy went on and on about how Fiona Barnes would manage being an older mum. Moira let a little smile slip across her face. She was delighted to hear that Helen was safe; she didn't need to worry about her now, but she needed to go back to bed. On her way up the stairs to her room, she looked out of the side hall window and could see the tips of the Barnes Farmhouse chimneys. There was a sadness inside her that she wasn't able to keep her baby, but there was a little feeling of happiness that the child was safe and warm.

Dragging her tired body up the last of the stairs, she got herself snuggled into bed. Falling into a deep sleep straight away.

TWO

BOBBY AND JOY

August 16th, 1967 - Moira's sixteenth birthday. She wanted a party but knew that would not happen. There had been a few small gifts waiting for her when she came down the stairs. The kitchen was bright; her mum and dad were doing their best to sing '*Happy Birthday*' but neither of them were ever going to make their fortunes making records!

Joy had wanted to give Moira more for her birthday, but it just wasn't possible. She looked across at her husband with a sliver of annoyance. Losing his job in Dumfries had been a blow they could not afford. They had met at a dance in Castle Douglas. He was tall and slim, with slicked-back black hair and the brightest blue eyes she had ever seen. Her heart had skipped a beat when he asked her to dance.

They were married that year, almost twenty-two years ago. Age had been kind to him. He was still a very handsome man. The years had not been so kind to her. They had waited six years for a child when Moira had unexpectedly arrived. She was so tiny and frail-looking, with a head full of dark curly hair.

Looking after a new baby had been a shock to the system for them both. Moira had been a colicky baby, but had soon grown into a delightful, happy toddler with a cheerful disposition she had deep set brown eyes and always looked so intense. Bobby was so good with her. Often, Joy would watch them from the kitchen window as they made their way up the lane to the woods. She chose not to go with them most of the time.

Sighing, she asked them both, "What would you like for your birthday breakfast?"

Moira was showing her dad the red handbag that Sally had given her for her birthday. She loved it; she squealed at the top of her voice, "Happy birthday to me."

It was nice to see her happy. Joy had noticed that she hadn't been her sunny self for a while and had put it down to the teenage blues.

After breakfast, Moira asked if she could go down to her best friend Sally's house.

"Of course you can, lass, enjoy yourself."

Bobby was happy to watch her skip away. He watched her as she made her way down the path, still so young at sixteen, swinging her red bag around. Settling back down to read his paper, he glanced at his wife as she busied herself sorting the kitchen. She had been a fine-looking woman when he first set eyes on her. He knew he wanted to marry her the night they met. Her long blonde curls and flashing green eyes were hard to resist.

The day they married was a beautiful spring day. In a simple ceremony with immediate family, they had said 'I do' promising to love and cherish each other forever. Four years later, he was not married to the same sweet, pretty girl. Joy's desperation for a child had taken over their lives. He dreaded listening to her weeping every month, knowing there was nothing he could do. There had been two times she thought she might have been pregnant, but both turned out to be false alarms.

Joy's bitterness at not being able to have children spilt over into being caustic about everyone else in the village. He was sad about not having children with his wife. He loved children. They had stopped talking about it; at this point in their relationship, they were only living together. That spark of first love had all but gone out. Two years later, when Moira had come into their lives, it was a blessing to have a distraction from his bitter wife. He adored his daughter. She was the light of his life.

Breaking into his thoughts, Joy's shrill voice shouted, "I'm off to clean the church."

Good, he thought, peace to read his Standard. Watching his wife's large frame disappear through the back door, he scooted into the living room to lie on the couch to read his paper.

Knowing that she would talk about him and anyone else who had put a foot wrong in the village with her church cronies annoyed him. He was tiring of the constant stream of bile that poured out of his wife's mouth. Her one passion in life was to find fault in everyone else but never in herself.

Thinking back to those early days with Moira, Joy had struggled to bond with her. Even though her deepest desire had been met, she couldn't get that mother and baby connection. Moira's arrival had been difficult for Joy to get her head around; still, he had thought she would be happier.

Joy struggled to care for Moira with the constant crying and being up at night. Often, she had thought about walking away from the whole situation. Struggling to care for Moira had become increasingly difficult. Some of the village women had to come in and help Joy with the baby and the house. Eventually, Joy found her feet and began to take care of both the house and Moira. They settled into a rhythm. Bobby often felt that his wife had never forgiven him for bringing Moira into their lives.

Things were never the same from then on. Their marriage had become barren, devoid of intimacy, yet he knew he had to stay for Moira's sake. As the years wore on and Joy became the opposite of her pretty name, Bobby just battened down the hatches and prayed that he could stay till Moira had grown up.

Bobby jolted out of a deep sleep and back into the living room to the sound of his daughter shouting, "Dad! Come here. Quickly."

He jumped off the couch and followed her to the kitchen, where his wife lay flat on her back, gasping for breath.

"Dad, Dad, do something."

He didn't know what to do. His wife's face froze into a contorted snarl, and she suddenly stopped moving.

Moira was yelling at him to do something; he shouted at her to run and get Dr Ottiwell. As she dashed out the back door, he knelt at the side of his wife's head; realising she was dead. Her eyes were wide open, and there was no sign of her breathing. What had happened to her? He wept quietly, kneeling there, saying some kind of garbled prayer for her soul as tears rolled down his face. Dr Ottiwell came rushing in the back door with Moira hot on his heels.

Moira was sent to the living room while Dr Ottiwell looked over her mum. *"What on earth had happened to her?"*, thought Moira, one minute she was chatting away, washing the dishes, the next thing she fell flat on her back. The crack of her head on the tiles was awful. Moira began to cry as Dr Ottiwell came through into the living room with her dad. Bobby knelt beside the chair. He took her hand in his and told her that her mum had died. Throwing herself at her dad, she cried. Bobby held his daughter tightly and let his own tears fall.

The following fortnight went by in a blur for Bobby and Moira. Villagers called in with food and cards. The ambulance had taken Joy to the big hospital in Dumfries. It had been a sudden massive stroke that had killed her; there was nothing anyone could have done. Moira was distraught. Now she had no mum, she was alone with her dad. Life for them had changed completely.

The funeral had been so hard. Many of Joy's church friends and villagers came to pay their respects. The cards and flowers were overwhelming. They rarely saw her mum's family, but it was nice to have seen them all at the funeral.

THREE

HELEN

Moira's little girl was growing into a bonny baby. She had caught a glimpse of her on many occasions at church and at the local grocer's, One time Mrs Barnes had asked her to hold the pram while she went into the post office to pay some bills. Moira felt her heart turn over looking at how beautiful her baby was. She put her hand into the pram and delighted at Helen gripping her finger.

Helen was now called Alice. Moira had drank in her baby's beautiful face in the pram that day at the Post Office and decided Alice was a good name for her to have. She had a thousand questions about her baby, but the fear of Mrs Barnes becoming suspicious stopped her. It might lead to her making a connection.

Moira's dad was lost. Bobby did not know what to do now. His wife had dropped dead. Moira was great at cooking and keeping the house tidy. Evenings at the local bar were the norm for him now. He hadn't been in the habit of going for a drink so often, but since his wife had died, he felt a sense of comfort being around people. Government benefits were keeping their heads above water, but deep down he knew he needed to find a job, and soon.

Moira sat at home most evenings on her own, listening to the radio or reading in her room. Since her mum had died, she felt very alone in her grief. Dad hardly uttered a word and usually returned home from the pub long after she had gone to bed which made her feel confused, unwanted and even more lonely. It felt like she had lost both her mum and her dad that day. She looked forward to weekends, it meant she could stay over at Sally's house. Chatting to her best friend allowed the grief to fade for a bit. Her dad would come and meet her after church on Sunday and walk her home. He no longer went to the church. The minister had called around twice after Joy had died, but Bobby had refused any invitations to come to church. He wasn't in the habit of going every week anyway, but he attended at Easter, Christmas, and other times. In contrast, Joy had gone every week, rain, hail or shine.

On one particular weekend, she and Sally had gone into town to go to the cinema. A late birthday present. Her birthday was ruined forever now. It had been almost two months since her mum had died. The film at the cinema was meant to be funny. It was called 'Where were you when the lights went out', which she thought was ironic when her mum's lights had literally just gone out. It was nice, though, to be out doing something different with Sally. On the way out of the cinema, she noticed a card in the box office window that read, 'Cashier wanted' She tapped on the window to enquire about the job. The little black blind flew up to reveal a flustered older woman, eager to give the job to Moira straight away.

Looking her up and down she said, "Can you start next Thursday?"

"Yes, yes I can, thank you," Moira replied.

She couldn't wait to get home and tell her dad the good news.

By the time Sally and Moira got home, it was getting dark. They had missed their usual bus while waiting for Moira to finish talking to the cashier about the job. Moira was exhausted. It had been a tough couple of months, but she was glad to have some good news to tell her dad.

Deciding to go home instead of staying at Sally's, she let herself in her back door, not being sure whether her dad would be home from the pub or not. However, he was home and sitting at the kitchen table.

"Where have you been?" he shouted as she came in.

She wasn't used to her dad shouting at her, but he seemed deeply upset with her.

"I told you I was going to the cinema tonight with Sally."

"You should have been home hours ago. I've been out of my mind sitting here worrying about where you were."

Moira was uncertain of him now; this angry dad was a new thing. She apologised and tried to shuffle past him to get to her bed. He grabbed her arm and pushed her hard against the kitchen press.

"Never come home this late again," he hissed in her face before letting her go.

She had never felt afraid of her dad before, but tonight there was a fire burning in his eyes that she had never seen before. There was a rage in that hissed threat that was new to her.

Why was he waiting on her, he knew she usually stayed at Sally's on Saturdays.

Was he drunk? Was it grief working its way out? Whatever it was, Moira knew it wasn't her dad. There was definitely something wrong.

Moira crept into her room, her legs shaking, making her steps wobbly. She flopped onto her bed and tried to stifle her tears. What's going on? What on earth is wrong with her dad? Her mum's death had completely changed him. She wanted to go downstairs and hug him, but she was afraid to. Should she tell someone that he wasn't coping? Sleep eventually overtook her.

Bobby woke up early as usual. As soon as the sun popped its head over the skyline, he opened his eyes, head thumping. Memories came flooding back of bumping into an old school friend in the bar the previous night. He knew he had drunk more than his usual half pint. He jolted upright as the stark, clear memory of grabbing Moira and pushing her against the press ran through his head. Why on earth had he grabbed at her like that? It was difficult to remember exactly what last night had been full of. Then he remembered a woman in his arms, kissing him and laughing outside the house. He was feeling mortified. He hoped that there weren't any more moments to remember. Bobby knew he had to speak to Moira before he left to start his new job at a farm on the other side of the village, or his conscience wouldn't settle.

Upstairs, Moira was hoping he would leave before she had to get up to go to the toilet. Unable to hold it in, she crept as quietly as she could to the bathroom, but he heard one of the old floorboards creak.

"Moira, come downstairs. I need to talk to you."

She loved her dad dearly, but was not enjoying this new dad since Joy had gone. She walked as slowly as she could downstairs to the kitchen, where, just like the night before, her dad was sitting at the kitchen table. He motioned to her to sit down.

"Moira, I'm so sorry I shouted at you last night. I had too much to drink, got home late, and you weren't home. I was afraid something had happened to you. My heart would break completely if something were to happen to you as well."

A tear rolled down Bobby's face, which caused Moira to burst into tears. They held onto each other for a few minutes, allowing their grief to work its way out.

Letting each other go, Moira asked her dad if he wanted her to make a cup of tea. "Yes please," he replied.

"I have something to tell you," said Moira excitedly.

Bobby was delighted to hear about the job at the box office. It would certainly help. Although it was only part-time, it would give Moira something else to focus on in the coming months. He had pledged to Moira that he would stay home on the nights she wasn't working in town.

"We need to be here for one another Moira," Bobby said.

"Yes Dad, we do," replied Moira as she reached out for another hug, before he left for work.

Moira slumped back down at the kitchen table. She thought about her baby every day. She thought she could switch off from it and pretend it never happened. Her thoughts turned to Helen at least once every day, nighttime was difficult as her thoughts would always turn to Helen. Helen's birthday was going to be the worst. She wanted to be the one delighting in watching her open gifts and play with them. She had been so afraid when she had her, and the memories of that night would not leave her alone. She had wondered if she could now tell her dad, but had quickly put that thought away. *"What good would that do? She could cope, and she got to see little Helen now and again in passing,"* she thought to herself.

Four

Tragedy Strikes

Fiona Barnes hummed quietly as she hung out her washing her mind full of the wonderful gift left on her doorstep. Her thoughts went to that special morning when she had risen early with stomach ache. In the silence of early morning, she heard footsteps rushing away from her back door interrupted by a bucket being kicked over. *"Someone is after the ducks,"* she thought. Opening the back door, she looked down and there on the step, she spotted a blanket with something in it. Her mind was racing. What should she do? Here was their deepest desire come true, but at the same time, this baby belonged to someone else. She brought the baby into the kitchen. She was warm and seemed healthy; she hadn't been out on the step for long. Who on earth would have been pregnant and not want the baby? Was the baby a gift from God? Fiona and her husband had prayed every night for years for a baby, and now there was a newborn baby girl in her arms.

Fiona rushed upstairs to show her husband Gavin the baby.

Their decision didn't take long; they were keeping the baby and calling her Alice, after Fiona's mother. There was the occasional worrying moment when Fiona thought about where her child had come from and what if her real mother turned up one day? There were no words for the joy she experienced hearing her little Alice squeal with delight, being lifted by her daddy and whirled about. She couldn't believe Alice had already been with them for over a year.

The back door was open, the sun was shining, and little Alice was in her baby walker, zipping around the flagged yard. A big red butterfly had caught Alice's attention, and she laughed as she zipped along trying to catch it. Fiona heard the wheels hit something and turned to see Alice fly out of the walker, hitting her head hard on the flags. The silence in that moment was deafening. All she could hear was her heart hammering in her chest. It felt like forever till she got to Alice. She knelt at her child's side, lifting her limp body close to hers.

"Alice, Alice, come on Alice, Mummy's here."

The tears streamed down her face as she pressed her baby close to her heart, knowing that she was gone. Gavin found her sitting in the backyard, Alice held tightly to her chest.

The ambulance came quickly to take Alice and Fiona to the hospital. The journey to the hospital was too short. Fiona did not want to let her child go to be looked over by the doctors. She didn't want to hear the words that her daughter was dead. Gavin heard her wailing long before he saw his wife. He was unsure how to comfort her; his own heart was broken by the loss of his beloved Alice and the broken heart of his wife. His thoughts were racing. He asked himself, *"Should we have handed Alice over to the authorities that morning when we found her on their back step? Is this God's way of punishing us?"*

The doctor arrived and explained that the blow to Alice's head was catastrophic; she wouldn't have survived it under any circumstances. The doctor went on to explain the dangers of baby walkers and then left them to console each other. Gavin put the medication he had been given for his wife in his jacket pocket and encouraged his wife to come home and leave Alice with the doctors till they could see to the funeral arrangements.

Fiona Barnes woke up at midday the next day. She had taken two of the strong sleeping tablets that had been prescribed for her. She sat up fast, making herself feel groggy; she strained to hear Alice and remembered instantly that Alice was gone. She made her way slowly downstairs to the kitchen where Gavin was sitting at the kitchen table looking dishevelled. She knew he hadn't slept all night. What were they to do? This was a tragedy far too complex for them; they had not only lost their own child but also someone else's child. The tears flowed as their eyes locked at that moment.

Moira had heard the ambulance go through the village but thought nothing of it. It was later on that evening that her dad took a call to tell him that the Barnes baby had died in a tragic accident. Moira knew the news wasn't good by the look on her dad's face. When he relayed the news to Moira, she could not get her head around it; her baby was dead, your baby is dead, was all her head was screaming back at her. She flew up the stairs as fast as she could and threw herself onto her bed and cried her heart out. The questions were bouncing off the insides of her mind. How? Where? When?

It was unbelievable. She knew she had to get a grip on her emotions, but the pain she was feeling was intense, she couldn't breathe almost causing her to choke, as she tried in vain to hold back the tears.

Bobby was surprised at his teenage daughter's reaction to the news of baby Alice's death. He could only put it down to how it hadn't been long since her mother had died, and maybe still had not dealt with that. She was almost seventeen, now a young woman. He was unsure as to whether he should go to her or leave her to come down herself. Leaving her was the best option in his mind. They could talk about it in the morning if she wanted to. Little did he know that it was his granddaughter who was lying in the mortuary in Dumfries's Cresswell hospital.

Bobby waited for Moira to come downstairs the following morning, but there was no sign of her; he hadn't heard her up and about either. Leaving her a note, he left for work. Moira was lying wide awake, waiting for him to leave the house. Her mind was racing around at one hundred miles an hour. Her baby was dead, dead, and she was in pieces, not being able to grieve in the way she wanted to. Why had this happened? Helen would be alive if she had taken her chances and brought the baby home that night. Too many what-ifs were flying around the inside of her head. She needed to get out of the house. The walls were caving in on her, and the cacophony of thoughts was becoming too much for her. She got dressed and shot out the back door, almost running in her haste to get a bit of space. Her legs and her hammering heart took her all the way to the woods where Helen had been born. She threw herself down to the ground and wept till there were no more tears left. She felt safe venting all that grief up there in the woods.

As Moira sat up, completely exhausted, she heard the soft crunch of the undergrowth; someone was making their way toward her. She put her back against the nearest tree and hardly dared to breathe. How would she explain her presence here in the woods and the state that she was in? She could make out the shape of a woman making her way along the little-used pathway.

Fiona Barnes was distraught; her baby was dead, and there was no getting away from that fact. They had registered her birth and named themselves as the parents. She desperately wanted to know to whom the baby belonged. Fiona and Gavin lived outside the village itself, their contact with villagers was infrequent, usually post office visits or shopping days. She wasn't too aware of all the families in the village and had tried to think of teenagers who could have been Alice's real mum. It had crossed her mind that it may have been someone passing through or someone who had made their way over here to have the baby. Why did they leave Alice on their doorstep? She had a niggling feeling it was someone who knew they would care for Alice. Someone who knew they desperately wanted children. But, who could that be?

Her head came up from her thoughts quickly at the crack of a twig. She got the feeling that someone was in the woods with her. Twigs cracked all the time in the woods with animals scurrying around. This was different!

She called out, "Is anyone there?"

She moved along the path a bit, peering into the greenery on each side, and said softly, "Hello,"

Moira knew straight away that it was Fiona Barnes. The blood was pumping so hard in her veins that she was sure Fiona could hear it. 'What should she do?' It was agonising waiting for her to move on. There was no way she could cope with any form of communication with Fiona right now or ever. After a few more whispered hellos, Fiona moved along the path away from Moira. Breathing a sigh of relief, Moira made her way out of the woods in the opposite direction.

As she reached the edge of the woods, Fiona knew that there had been someone in the undergrowth, but soon realised that whoever was in there did not want to be seen. She blushed as she imagined that maybe she had stumbled upon a courting couple. They must be mortified, she smiled to herself, remembering her own courting days with Gavin.

Moira thought she was going to burst; she had held her breath for so long. "*Thank God Fiona had moved on,*" she thought.

Moira made her way back home. Her thoughts turned to Fiona who she knew would be devastated after all she had brought Alice up for fifteen months. Helen … Alice … Alice … Helen …. Confusion, turmoil and endless grief choked Moira. Letting herself in the back door, she made her way up the stairs knowing she needed a bath. She felt dirty from being in the woods, and wanted to try and settle her fragile thoughts. Moira crept back into her bed and lay there with her thoughts racing round her head. She heard her dad come in from work. She sat bolt upright when she heard him come in. She knew he would be worried about her after last night. She pulled on her housecoat and joined him in the kitchen. She had to avoid being caught out.

Bobby was surprised to see Moira was still in her housecoat. She was as white as a sheet. He assumed it must be that 'time'. 'Would you like something from Sandy's Chippy for tea, love?'

He was glad to hear her say, "Yes, please."

He asked her to set the table while he went for the chippy. Moira desperately wanted to tell him about Helen. She knew however deep down it would serve no purpose except to make her feel better, not having to carry her secret.

The funeral of her baby came and went. Moira chose not to go; but the following day she laid a posy of flowers at her baby's grave and said her goodbyes. She had to get away from the village. The memories were too much to bear. The guilt was weighing heavily on her mind, and the deceit ate away at her inside. Just looking at her dad every day, knowing that she couldn't tell him that his granddaughter lay just yards from him, was becoming too much for her to carry.

Moira started to think about how to get out of the village and away from the memories. As much as she may have wanted to, there was no way that she could confess to her dad what had happened. In a way, she thought that it was probably a good thing that her mum was not here anymore, as she would have definitely sniffed out that something was amiss. The tears began to flow again; she had not cried as much in all of her life. She was deeply sorry for the mess that had unfolded over the last couple of weeks. She even felt guilty for causing the Barnes family so much grief.

She had seen them both around the village. Seeing their grief-stricken faces had made her scuttle off without even saying hello.

Moira headed out of the house for some fresh air. After walking through the village, she found herself heading out to the Barnes House instead of turning towards her own home. As she walked slowly through the village, she spotted Mrs Pines in the sweet shop;

she waved and smiled. Mrs Pines, a small, wizened-looking old lady had the speed of a gazelle, should you try to touch any of the sweets on the counter in her shop. She had always been there, with no husband or children that Moira was aware of. Fond memories of a Saturday treat passed through her head. A couple of houses down was Sandy's chip shop which nowadays only opened in the evening from 4 pm to 8 pm, but never on a Sunday. Sandy stood outside having a smoke.

"Alright, there, young lass, what's the long face for?" he had shouted. She hadn't realised that her face was looking so long.

She had replied, "I've not got a long face, Sandy, I have a square face."

She had smiled at him as she continued on her way out of the village. She wondered briefly what the village would have made of the whole Alice/Helen story.

Reaching the Barnes house, she waited by the wall for a few moments before swinging the gate open and walking in. Her heart was hammering in her chest. What was she thinking about? She hoped that Fiona Barnes was home alone. The gate clanged back on itself, causing her to jump. Racing to the back door before she could change her mind, she took a deep breath and knocked.

Fiona Barnes had just finished doing the ironing, listening to the Beatles belting out their latest hit. She heard the knock at the door and thought to herself that it was strange. No one really called at her house unannounced. Seeing Moira Kirkwell standing there was a bit of a surprise. She knew that her mum had passed away suddenly not so long ago, but didn't really know the family well at all.

"Moira, how nice to see you. Is everything ok with you and your dad?"

The next thing she knew, Moira was in her arms, in floods of tears. What on earth was wrong with the girl? Fiona held her until the tears subsided a bit, then brought her through to the kitchen. Thankfully,

Gavin was out at the market in town. Trying to work out what was troubling this young girl, she thought maybe something had happened to her dad.

"Sit down, dear, sit down. Moira, what's wrong? Is your dad alright?"

The tears kept flowing, and Moira couldn't speak.

Eventually, Moira blurted out, "Helen's dead. I'm so sorry."

Sobbing uncontrollably, she threw her arms around Fiona.

She held the girl at arm's length and said, "Moira, who is Helen?"

With huge tears rolling down her face, Moira looked straight into Fiona's eyes and said, "Helen is Alice."

Fiona's eyes were like saucers, "It was you, Oh my gosh, Moira, Alice was your baby."

Moira whimpered a quiet, "Yes," burying her face in her hands.

Fiona could hardly believe what she was hearing "Does anyone else know?"

"Nobody," Moira whispered, bursting into fresh tears.

FIVE

SALLY

Sally Moffat was busy making dinner; her mum had taken a twilight shift at the mill. Sally loved cooking. At seventeen, she was tall and curvy with straight blonde hair. All the local boys were always trying to impress her. She just wasn't interested. Poetry and music were her two passions. She heard the back door open. *"Who could that be,"* she thought. In waltzed Moira, her best friend in the whole world. They had been besties since they could remember.

"Moira, where have you been hiding?"

Happy to see her friend, she gave Moira a great big hug. Where Sally was fair, Moira was dark. Where Moira was short, Sally was tall, Moira was chubby, and Sally was slim. They were complete opposites. Their friendship was closer than sisters. Sally was delighted to see Moira.

"I'm just making some dinner, do you want some?"

Moira knew Sally was a great cook.

"Yes, please," said Moira happily.

They sat at the dinner table, eating a lovely chicken salad with boiled potatoes, while the radio played one of her favourite songs, Hey Jude.

"What's up, Moira?"

Sally knew her friend had had something on her mind for the past few weeks, but she wasn't sure what. She just assumed it was her trying to work through her mother's sudden death. It had shocked the whole village at the time. But Sally could see that Moira was troubled.

"Nothing's up, I'm just bored with village life, I really want to move away and see the world," Moira said wistfully.

"Wow! Big statement there, Moira. What brought that on then?"

"I feel trapped, hemmed in here, Sally."

"What about your dad, Moira?"

Moira thought about her dad all the time.

"What about my dad? He will be fine, he has his friends, and I think he might be happy to see me spread my wings a bit, and see more of life than this tiny village."

"Where would you go?" asked Sally, "Glasgow? England? The possibilities are endless."

Moira had already spoken to her boss at the box office. She knew they had cinemas in a few places, and a transfer would work well if a job became available in one of them. She filled Sally in about her plan.

"So you could end up anywhere really, have you spoken to your dad about it yet?" Sally asked. That was something she hadn't done yet, but it needed to be said sooner rather than later.

They scooted up to Sally's room and spent the evening talking about fashion and their favourite boys and pop stars. They laughed over some of the silly things they had done over the years.

Bobby made his way home from the pub, hoping that Moira had made him some dinner. He was tired and hungry. Starting a new job the week before had been a significant boost after his wife's untimely death. He really couldn't believe she was gone; it all happened so quickly. Moira had been in shock for weeks after it. She seemed a bit more like herself these days.

She would be eighteen soon. His baby was going to be an adult. How did that happen? It was 1969, and times were changing. What was next for his daughter? She was bright and should be looking for opportunities outside the village. He would have moved given half a chance, but his wife had never considered moving.

Moira bounced in the back door just after 10 pm, full of plans. Her dad was sitting at the kitchen table reading the paper.

"Hi Dad, would you like a cup of tea?"

"Yes, that would be nice," Bobby said.

He watched his daughter as she busied herself with getting cups and the teapot ready for tea.

"Moira, I was wondering if there would be anything special you would like for your eighteenth birthday?"

She stopped in her tracks to think about it. *"I haven't thought about it, Dad."* She sat down, looking at the pretty orange cups with their matching teapot, waiting a few minutes for the tea to brew; none of them liked a pale cup of tea. She decided to use his question as an opportunity to ask about moving away.

"Dad, I know what I would like for my eighteenth birthday. I would love it if you would allow me to move away from the village with my job. They have said that they can help me find lodgings if I want a job at one of their other cinemas. What do you think, Dad?"

Bobby had always known that one day Moira would want to fly the nest and thought that he was reasonably well prepared for it. He wasn't! To hear her say that she had already made plans with her job to go somewhere else hurt his heart. He would have to let her go.

"Moira, you go with my blessing, but always know that you will always have a home to come back to if it doesn't work out."

Moira breathed a sigh of relief.

"Aw Dad, thanks, I really want to get away from the village, there is a big, world out there for me to discover. I want to go and make memories to share them all with you, Dad."

Bobby was proud of the young woman she had become. He would enjoy listening to her stories of new places.

Moira went to bed that night full of plans, thoughts of the future, moving away, wow! She could hardly believe it; her dad had said yes to her moving away. She had thought he might say no. She felt that he would hate being alone in the house. Moira had some savings from all the nights she had worked at the box office, so money wasn't going to hold her back.

Bobby went to bed with a heavy heart, already feeling the pain of losing his daughter, his one and only child, to the big, wide world out there. He wasn't happy for her; he knew it would be tough out there and hoped she would be home fairly quickly. He had a little money put by and would make sure that she always had enough wherever she was.

Six

Moving Away

Two months later, she was chasing Sally down the street to tell her the good news.

"Sally, Sally! Slow down," Moira shouted, "I have to tell you something, you won't believe it."

"What is it?" asked Sally.

"It's Leeds," Moira gasped. "I'm heading off to Leeds, there is a position in the Leeds cinema."

Sally looked at her friend and saw the elation on her face. Moira was beaming from ear to ear at the thought of moving so far away. *"What was the big problem with the village anyway,"* Sally thought? She was not looking forward to her friend moving and had even prayed at church that she wouldn't be transferred to another cinema. God was obviously not listening to her that was for sure. They had chatted about moving away together, but Sally wasn't ready to move away from her mum or the village yet.

Rushing back home after spending the afternoon with Sally, Moira got straight to making her dad his favourite dinner. He loved corned beef hash; Moira hated it. She had never liked corned beef. She put a pan of boiled potatoes on for herself; mashed potatoes with lashings of butter were one of her favourites. Her dad looked tired when he came in the door. Moira could not contain her excitement as soon as the dinner was on the table.

"I'm going to Leeds, Dad, Leeds, a big city in the north of England."

Bobby knew where Leeds was; it was nearly 160 miles away. He did his best to smile at her.

He asked her, "When will you be leaving, Moira?

"My job starts in three weeks, but I need to go down the week before to settle in." Moira gushed.

Bobby looked across at her. He could see she was delighted to have this new job. Where had his little girl gone?

Moira had so much to do. People to see and tell the news to, and memories to make with Sally and her dad before she went. She felt nervous about the big move but knew she had to get away from the village to help her move on. She would feel sad at moving away from all that she had known all of her life, and she wondered if she would manage to settle in somewhere else.

Being a confident, clever girl, she knew that the job would be something she could do. It was moving into digs and finding her way around a new place that made her tummy turn over when she thought about it.

Before she started her new job, her boss had given her a week off to give her time to pack and make the journey to Leeds, and she would have time to find her way around. Moira had decided that a picnic with Sally, Patsy, and her dad would be nice. She wondered how her dad was feeling about it all. Tonight, she would spend time with him and ask him to be honest.

Moira gave Sally a call, "What do you think about a picnic with us all before I head off to Leeds. Your mum, my dad, and us two?"

"Sounds good to me." Sally was not looking forward to Moira leaving.

They chatted for a while about the news and laughed about Mrs Wimpler, who had got her foot stuck in a drain, the highlight of the week in village life. No one could work out how she managed to do it; eventually, the fire brigade had come out from Dumfries to cut the drain cover off her foot, big news in their tiny world. Still smiling as she put the phone down, Moira went up to her room and gazed out at the woods.

"Bye-bye, Helen," she whispered.

"Dad, do you want egg sandwiches or cheese?"

Moira was busy making the sandwiches for the picnic she had organised, before she left for Leeds. Her dad was coming along too. It was looking like it would be a fantastic day. The sun was out, and a nice easterly breeze was blowing the washing that she had hung out on the line half an hour earlier. Moira felt great; she was looking forward to getting away from the village. She loved where she lived, but knew that she wanted to experience more in her life.

"Egg, please, Moira," her dad shouted, shaking her out of her thoughts.

The eggs were boiling anyway because she knew her dad would say egg. She was going to miss her dad and would worry a lot about him being on his own. She finished off the cheese sandwiches and poured cold water over the boiled eggs to make the shells come off more easily. A little tip her mum had taught her.

Moira dressed in jeans and a yellow blouse and packed her blue cardigan just in case the breeze got cooler. They left the house together and headed up the hill behind it. There was a nice, flat, green area up there with a few trees for shade if needed. Getting to the top, she could see that Patsy and Sally were already there. Moira felt a pang of sadness for Sally; her dad was rarely around, as he worked all over the world. It was good to see them, especially Patsy; Moira was very fond of Sally's mum and had always wanted a mum like Patsy. Growing up, Moira had always thought Sally was lucky to have a happy mum.

They laughed together and told stories of fond and sad memories of the past eighteen years in the village. Patsy and Bobby shared older stories that made the girls laugh out loud and give the odd 'Ooooh, really' with lots of giggles.

Packing up the picnic basket and making their way back down the hill, Moira looked around, so many memories, she could see the woods, the Barnes house and the village. Bobby had brought up the death of the Barnes baby, as he called her, while they were chatting. Moira felt a pang of sadness, but obviously couldn't show it, so she busied herself pouring drinks when her dad had started talking about it. Leaving little Helen behind was going to be hard.

Moving away was the answer for her. She put all the picnic stuff away, thinking to herself, when would it be used again? Maybe her dad would meet someone else; he wasn't that old, and he was still such a handsome man. She had church tomorrow, and the minister would pray for her before she left. It was a nice gesture, but Moira wasn't really sure if there was a god. Monday morning, she would be starting her journey to Leeds to begin her new life.

The church was just part and parcel of their lives in the village; most villagers attended the Sunday service, whether they believed or not. There were the odd few who didn't participate. The minister was nice; he didn't have a wife or family. Bobby and Moira usually sat relatively near the back. Moira's mum had been a true churchgoer; she went to the prayer meetings and other social gatherings the church had on. Bobby and Moira just attended, now and again, doing their best to listen without falling asleep. Moira wondered why they still went at all, since it was only really because of her mum's insistence that she went as a child. After the service ended, they went through the obligatory handshaking and back-patting on the way out. The minister was outside as they came out and stepped up to greet them.

"Mr Kirkwell and Moira, how are you both? You're leaving us Moira for pastures new? I hope you take the time to find somewhere to worship in Leeds."

"Yes, I will do," Moira felt a pang of guilt for lying.

"I leave tomorrow," Moira said.

He clasped her hand and said sincerely, "God will be with you, and please call me if you need me."

It was an awkward exchange as Moira didn't know the minister very well, but she felt strangely comforted by his words.

He turned to Bobby and said, "And for you, Mr Kirkwell, we will be keeping Moira in our prayers, and I do hope we continue to see you when you can come along, and if you ever need me, I will be right here. Don't hesitate to call me."

"Thank you, I will keep that in mind," Bobby said, knowing full well the next time he saw the minister, it would be at a wedding or a funeral.

Both Moira and Bobby were glad of the exchange between themselves and the minister; he was a good man and cared about what was going on in their lives.

The alarm clock went off at 6 am with great gusto, waking Moira up with a start. She had struggled to get to sleep, checking her case every five minutes to make sure she had everything she needed. Today was the big day; she was booked on the two o'clock train leaving from Dumfries. That meant she needed to be on the twelve o'clock bus to Dumfries. She had one place to go before she left the village. She had planned to go and plant a small tree where she had given birth to Helen/ Alice. She had nurtured the seedling for a few weeks. A rowan tree. She had read somewhere that they were used for protection. She wanted to protect the spot where she had been when her little girl had been born.

She set off quietly; she didn't want her dad to hear her leaving the house. It was eerily quiet in the woods. She thought back to that dreadful, life-changing night; she could hardly believe that it had actually happened. She had given birth, and her baby had died just over a year later. No one knew except her and Fiona Barnes, and that really affected her. She felt so guilty about it all. Taking a few moments at the spot, she planted the little rowan tree. She had tied a loose piece of green leather around it, in case she couldn't find it when she came back.

Walking back through the woods, she was surprised to see the minister heading toward her. What was he doing in the woods this early?

"Good morning, Moira," he waved cheerily at her as he approached.

"Good morning," she replied. "What are you doing up here in the woods this early?"

"I'm going to visit Mrs Barnes later on, so I thought I would have a walk through the woods as I pray my morning prayers. How about you, Moira? What are you doing out here so early?"

Moira wondered briefly what he would say if she told him she was planting a Rowan tree in memory of her dead daughter.

She just cheerily replied, "I'm just saying goodbye to eighteen years of memories before I leave for Leeds."

As she walked away, she took a long look at the spot where she had planted the tree. What was ahead for her? What would she like about being away from home? Would her dad be okay? She had to push the questions to the back of her mind for now; she had an adventure ahead. It really was the best for her to move.

Sitting on the bus to Dumfries with her dad on the pavement waiting for it to leave was so hard, inside she was feeling deep anxiety for herself and for him. He looked so alone standing there, in his brown coat and cap. He was a tall man. She was so proud of him. She wondered what he was really thinking under that cap. It must be killing him inside to be waving me off, but he's willing to let me fly. Tears began to pool at the side of her eyes. The bus jerked as it began to pull away, and she waved frantically at him, trying to smile her best smile.

Bobby didn't see the tears in Moira's eyes because of the tears in his eyes. He loved his precious daughter so much. He didn't want her to move away, but he felt that if he had tried to stop her and make her stay when she clearly had wings that wanted to fly, it would have been disastrous.

The times are changing so fast these days. He prayed silently that no harm would come to her on this big adventure. He hoped she would make good friends and meet good people. He was going to visit her in a month with Patsy and Sally.

Patsy and Sally came flying up the street towards the bus as it was pulling away. They had said they couldn't see her off because of an appointment, but here they were waving and blowing kisses. Moira couldn't stem the tears as she saw her best friend and her mum. She was glad they couldn't really see her.

Of course, she was nervous; it was a big move. She knew that she had to make the best of Leeds. Knowing, of course, that she could come home at any point.

Sally was sad to see her friend go. They had been friends since childhood, they had gone through school together, they had laughed together, they had cried together, and they knew everything about each other. Well, Sally thought she knew everything about Moira, but Moira had never been able to share with Sally about Helen.

The bus trip and the train ride to Leeds were fairly uneventful; she had no problems with her connection at Dumfries. The train to Leeds was busy but not overly so; she managed to get a seat to herself. It didn't take too long to get to Leeds. She got off the train and looked at the note with the address she needed to reach. It looked easy enough to find; it wasn't too far from the station. She asked at the ticket office if they knew where the address was. A lady looked at the note, shook her head, and said no, she hadn't heard of that address.

Thinking she might have saved a few bob by making her own way there, she realised the best thing to do instead was get a taxi from the station.

The taxi pulled up at the first house on a grimy-looking street. The houses were all packed together on both sides of the street. They were tall red brick buildings, with chimneys belching out smoke. She paid the taxi driver, he helped her get her case out of the boot and waved a cheery goodbye. Knocking on the door, Moira felt a stab of fear. What if she didn't like it here? It didn't look very friendly from the outside.

Hearing footsteps making their way to the grubby door she was looking at, she was surprised to see an older lady with a broad, welcoming smile answer the door.

"Come in, Moira, we have been expecting you."

Moira looked around at the long hallway. The floor had red-patterned linoleum and a threadbare rug.

"Did you find us alright, dear?" she said.

"Yes, thank you, I got a taxi from the station," Moira replied.

"I'm Barbara, and this is Francis," she said with a flourish of her hand as they walked into the sitting room together.

Francis hardly took the time to glance up from his paper to look at the new lodger.

"Hello," he grunted from behind the pages.

"Don't worry about him, dear."

Moira wasn't worried about him; she was worried about this whole adventure. Her stomach was grumbling and full of butterflies at the same time.

"You must be famished. Would you like a sandwich and some tea?" Barbara asked.

"Yes, please," Moira was feeling very hungry.

"Well, sit yourself down there, and let's get you sorted. We can look at your room once you have eaten. How does that sound?"

Barbara left her sitting there with Francis while she made the sandwich.

Moira was feeling a bit disoriented; time was all over the place. Looking up at the clock on the wall, she was surprised to see it was already five fifteen.

Barbara returned fairly quickly with some sandwiches and a pot of tea. Sitting down in the chair opposite Moira, she began asking Moira questions about herself. She asked her what job she had and about her parents and siblings. Moira explained that she only had her dad and that her mum had died suddenly a couple of years earlier. Barbara told her that she had been running the guest house for seven years now and had met some lovely people along the way.

"There are five guests here now that you have arrived. It's lovely to have a young woman for a change, too," said Barbara with a smile.

Sandwiches and tea finished, Barbara led the way upstairs to her room, with Francis following behind with her bags. Opening the door and handing Moira the keys, she pointed out the rule book on the small, brown bedside cabinet.

"Now, Moira, we have rules in the house that are all in the book there. Anything you don't understand, come and find me, and I hope you can settle in ok."

Stepping into the room, she could see it was pretty basic, a small single bed, an old-fashioned dark wooden wardrobe and a chest of drawers. The bedside cabinet had a lamp with a bright pink shade with little pom poms dangling around the entire bottom edge of it.

The floor was covered with a dark, patterned linoleum, with a rug that had seen better days. She was feeling homesick already. The window in her room looked out into the street; it was nothing like the beauty of where she had come from.

She knew it was going to be different, but now that she was here, she was feeling like turning around and going straight back home. No, Moira, come on, buckle up. You can do this, trying desperately to convince herself to stay, she started to unpack and put away her clothes and things.

By the time she had done all of that, she was feeling tired. It was 8.30 pm, too early to go to bed. But tired enough to get ready for bed. She went to the bathroom to wash and brush her teeth. Slipping into the nice, clean sheets on her bed, she got the rule book and started to read. It was all fairly straightforward. She was glad that breakfast was part of the tenancy deal.

Moira woke with a start, knocking the rule book to the floor. She had fallen fast asleep reading the rules. Looking at the clock on the wall, it was 7.30 am, and breakfast finished at 8.30 am. Jumping out of bed, she grabbed her toiletry bag and headed off down the hall to get washed and ready for the day ahead. Choosing her outfit carefully, she put on her purple cords and brown roll-neck jumper. She had today to explore her new surroundings before she started her new job.

GETTING TO KNOW LEEDS

Moira wondered what her first day might be like. Thinking about what it would be like with new workmates and a new boss. The walk to her work, it was not long, but thirty minutes would not be great if it were raining. Today was nice and cool, perfect for exploring and working out her route.

Just making it into the breakfast room for twenty past eight, she helped herself to some toast and tea. Barbara bustled in and asked if she would like a bacon barm.

"What's a barm?" Moira asked.

"It's a bread roll, Moira," said Barbara with a smile; she had many lodgers flummoxed with that one.

She had brought her coat and bag down to the breakfast room to save her the long climb back up the stairs. Slipping her jacket on, she stepped outside into the cool morning. Barbara had given her clear instructions on how to reach the cinema. She estimated half an hour, but she arrived twenty minutes later outside the side door of the Majestic. That was easy, she said to herself. No need to worry about tomorrow now.

She made her way into the town centre and had a good look around the shops. Leeds was busy, a vast change from her little village. Even Dumfries was tiny in comparison.

Buying herself a sandwich and a drink for lunch, she sat on a bench near the shops, watching all the people dashing around doing their shopping. Mums with prams, men, smoking, walking, with their hands in their pockets, elderly couples linking arms, moving at their own pace. Everyone was a stranger to her.

It felt odd not knowing anyone who walked past. She hoped she would make some friends down here. Looking around wistfully she wished Sally was here with her. Popping her litter in the nearest bin, she made her way back to the lodgings. Once back at the street she was staying in, she wandered around the adjoining streets to familiarise herself with where she was. There was a park two streets down with some small children running around, screeching and laughing. It was nice to watch for a few minutes.

Letting herself in the front door, she was met by a man dashing out. He was tall with red hair, which was all she managed to make out; he was going that fast.

Barbara was in the living room watching TV with Francis.

"I see you bumped into Brian then," said Barbara.

"Yes, he was in a right hurry, wasn't he?" said Moira.

"Aye, always in a hurry, that one," Francis grunted.

"How's your day been then, Moira. Did you find the cinema alright?"

Moira replied, "Yes, nice and easy to find, thank you, and I had a mooch round the city centre and around here to get my bearings."

"What are you doing for your tea, Moira?" Barbara asked.

"I'm going to the chippy on the corner for a treat tonight, then I will get shopping in for the rest of the week." Moira was looking forward to some fish and chips.

The kitchen area was open for tenants to make their own tea; each had a cupboard to store food and other items, and a shelf in one of the two fridges.

Feeling a bit more settled, Moira asked Barbara where the nearest phone box was. She wanted to call her dad to let him know she was ok.

"It's three streets down on the corner. Make sure you have plenty of change," Barbara answered.

"Thanks, Barbara, I brought a pile of change with me," Moira said as she headed out of the front door.

Walking round to the phone box, Moira was checking out the streets around her. It was a grimy-looking place, but people she had passed had nodded a friendly hello.

Bobby was delighted to hear from her. She sounded happy enough. Barbara seemed to be nice. He wished her well, starting the new job in the morning.

"I love you, Moira."

"I love you too, Dad."

Putting the receiver down, she felt for her dad so far away on his own; she hoped that his friends in the village would make sure he was ok.

Moira had been awake since six thirty. Dressed and down for breakfast by seven thirty. Far too early, she didn't start till twelve. Nerves were kicking in now.

Walking to the cinema, she rehearsed what she was going to say. Hi, I'm Moira, the idiot from Scotland. She made herself laugh with some of the lines she was making up.

Knocking on the side door as she had been instructed, it felt like she waited forever for the door to open.

A thin, pale-looking tall young man, with a shock of tousled blonde hair, opened the door and snarled at her, "What do you want?"

Flashing her best smile, she looked him straight in the eye and said, "I'm Moira. I start here as a cashier today."

"You'd best come in then," banging the door behind him and slamming the bolt home, he growled, "Follow me."

The cinema was dark and dingy. Moira could smell the musty, old smell of the carpets as she walked through the front foyer.

"Wait here. I will go and get Mr Stewart."

She watched the young man head down the foyer to a bright yellow door, with the word 'office' on it.

She walked around the foyer, gazing at the big movie posters. As part of her job package, she could see any film she wanted. She had enjoyed watching films at the Dumfries cinema.

"Ah, Moira, how very nice to meet you," boomed Mr Stewart's broad northern voice.

"Follow me if you will. We can discuss your role. I see you met Billy, my son."

Not knowing what to say, Moira scuttled after him as he strode towards a pale blue door in the foyer; she hadn't noticed that door when she came in. She found herself in a tiny room with a table and two chairs. Mr Stewart gestured to her to sit in one of them.

"You'll know the ropes, Moira. Not much different here, we are all one big happy family, your first shift will start at 12 sharp, and just so you know, we don't tolerate tardiness here."

"I'm looking forward to getting on with my shift," Moira said confidently.

Mr Stewart was a big man, as broad as he was long, which was something her mum used to say. His voice was loud, too. Her boss at Dumfries had been a quietly spoken older woman.

"Let's start you in the box office today, Moira,"

Mr Stewart let her know their meeting was finished by striding out of the door.

"*Gosh, he was a bit of a character,*" she thought to herself.

Making her way to the box office, Billy was standing beside the door waiting to let her in. He had a bag of change for her to count and put in the little change drawers. It was a busy afternoon, and she was glad to clock off at 4 pm. Billy appeared from nowhere with a bag to put the takings in. Once it was all counted and safely in the bag, Billy locked the door to the box office.

Shift one was over, and nobody had died. Mr Stewart was loud and big, Billy was thin and quiet, and the usherette Caroline was a lovely lady, she guessed maybe in her forties.

Stepping out into the street, she realised that she was very hungry. After a few minutes of walking, she found a lovely cafe. She decided to have a plate of sausage and mash with a hot cup of coffee. Looking around at the other customers, she wondered if anyone else was feeling a bit lonely.

Moira wished she were closer to home. She missed Sally and her dad so much.

She would be getting paid on Fridays and had promised to call them both on Friday night or Saturday morning, depending on what shift she was on. She had her rota for the next two weeks; she would write to them both tonight and let them know to be in for her calling.

As she got up to leave, the waitress came over to take her cup and plate.

The waitress asked, "I haven't seen you here before? Are you visiting someone?"

She was young, with her short blond hair in a bob.

"I've moved here to work at the Majestic," said Moira, smiling at the girl.

"You have a lovely accent, where are you from?"

Moira explained she was from a small village called Glendoon, twenty miles outside of Dumfries, near the Scottish borders.

"Welcome to Leeds," she said with a cheery smile.

Moira smiled back and made her way out of the cafe.

Making her way back to the house, Moira thought to herself that the cafe might be a place to go again; the waitress seemed nice.

It was a long week at work with plenty of ups and downs. Cheeky little boys trying to sneak in for free, people trying to get in without the right money, but nothing much got past Billy.

Billy was the same age as Moira. He was so quiet; he never really said much. She wondered if it was because his dad was so loud. Over the course of the week, she had found out they had run the cinema since he was a baby. He had spent his childhood around the cinema. They had a small flat at the back of the building. Like Moira, Billy's mum had passed away a few years ago.

Walking home on Friday afternoon, she was looking forward to calling Sally and her dad. She had plenty of change from the box office that she had asked Mr Stewart for in her wages. Letting herself into the house, she made her way up to her room with tired legs. Throwing herself onto the bed and kicking her shoes off, she let out a whoop of delight. She was off tomorrow and looking forward to going into town.

Popping her rent money into an envelope, she headed back downstairs in jeans and an orange jumper, and headed out to the phone box.

She dialled her dad's number carefully. She was glad to hear his cheery, "Hello, Moira, how are you? What is it like down there?"

Her dad was full of questions.

"Slow down, Dad," she laughed.

"I'm doing well, Dad, I'm enjoying working at the cinema, fed up seeing the same films over and over though," she reassured him that the lodgings were great, Barbara was lovely, and yes, she was eating well.

Her dad sounded tired. She wondered if he was ok. Ten minutes of chit-chat about the residents of the village was enough for Moira.

"I'm going to phone Sally now, Dad. You take care of yourself, bye, love you."

"Love you, Moira, bye."

She waited until she heard the click of the receiver going down, and put hers down too before dialling Sally's number.

"Hey, Moira, how's the big city then?" said Sally, glad to hear Moira's voice on the phone.

Moira spent a full twenty minutes chattering about her work, her digs, her walk to work and her boss and his son. Ending the call with, "Promise you will send me a letter, Sally."

"Of course, I will, Moira," Sally replied.

Promising to write back, Moira put the phone down with a heavy heart. She wasn't about to tell her dad or Sally that she was actually feeling very homesick. Collecting the coins she hadn't used and putting them in her jeans pocket, she made her way back to her digs.

Barbara was busy dusting and sweeping the floors. Moira wondered if Barbara had children.

Trudging up the stairs, a pang of sadness washed over her as she thought about little Helen. The what-ifs were running around her mind. Would Helen be alive today if she had only been brave enough to tell her parents she was pregnant? She would never know what difference that would have made, and that made her feel even worse.

Pulling open the little drawer of her side cabinet, she fished out her notepad and pen. Sally's mum had gifted her two sets of Basildon Bond writing pads with envelopes. Sally had given her a pretty red pen with a flower sticker. Setting about writing to her dad and Sally, ready to post in the morning, she tried to sound happy and hopeful to let them know they didn't need to worry about her.

She opened her bedroom window and lay down on the bed with her feet crossed over and her hands behind her head. She listened to the sounds of the house and the street. It was a stark contrast to her room at home, where all she heard was the kettle boiling and birds twittering. Had she done the right thing coming so far away? What was there for her at home? She knew she wanted more out of life than her mother had had. She didn't want to end up bitter and angry, trapped in a marriage she wasn't happy in.

Waking up with a start, Moira couldn't believe she had fallen asleep. Looking at the little blue alarm clock she had bought, she realised she had slept for nearly two hours. It was dark outside. Feeling chilly, she shut the room window. As she did so, she saw a young man in a hat leaving the house. She didn't recognise him from breakfast. Maybe he was a new guest.

Hungry, she realised she hadn't bought any shopping and had nothing in her cupboard space downstairs that would do for supper. Chips, it was then she said to herself. She had treated herself to a fish supper her first night here. Popping her coat back on, she set off to get herself a portion of chips. *Kirbys* was busy, obviously, it was well-liked being this busy on a Friday night. The queue was out the door.

She spotted the guy she had seen leaving the house earlier; he must be in the same boat, she thought. People were chattering to each other around her. It made her more aware that she was not a local. Smiling tentatively to one or two of the older ladies, she thought it best to say nothing with her Scottish accent. Not realising that when the young girl looked at her and shouted, everyone would hear her accent.

"A bag of chips, please," she said as quietly as she could.

"Speak up, love, what did you say?" The lady hadn't heard her.

She repeated her order in a louder voice. Feeling very self-conscious, she stepped away from the counter to wait for her order with her head down.

A slight tap on her shoulder made her turn round to see the young man with the red hair from the guest house smiling at her.

"I'm Brian. I saw you coming into Barbara's the other day."

Relaxing into a smile, Moira was so happy to hear another Scottish accent.

"Where are you from, Brian?" asked Moira.

Before he had a chance to reply she blurted out, "I'm Moira. I've come down from Dumfries."

"Oh, very nice, Moira. I hail from the big city of Glasgow."

They chatted a bit while they waited for their food.

EIGHT

FALLING IN LOVE

The weeks went on. Moira was enjoying her job at the cinema; she felt safe and comfortable in her lodgings. She had many a chat with Barbara in the evenings when she wasn't on shift. She had noticed that Barbara waited up for her when she was on a late shift.

She was getting along with Brian, too. They had made it a bit of a thing to go for a fish supper on Friday evenings. He was twenty-two and working on a contract in Leeds for a communications company. His parents had both passed away when he was fifteen. Fending for himself was something he had got used to fairly quickly. Like Moira, he was an only child.

When she shared with Brian about her mum dying so suddenly, it brought with it an unexpected wave of emotion. They had been walking back from the chippy, and he had put his arm around her shoulders and pulled her close. The closeness had felt good. Brian was a nice guy. He had asked her lots of questions about her family over the past few weeks. It was nice building a friendship with him.

The warmer months had set in, and the nights were longer. Things were good. Coming home one Wednesday evening, Moira found a letter pushed under her door. *"Who's this from?"* she thought to herself. Opening the letter, she read:

Dear Moira,

I have very much enjoyed our Friday night chats and fish suppers. I would like to know if you would step out with me on an official date one evening. We could go to a restaurant or to the cinema on Saturday.

Moira was delighted; she really liked him. She quickly wrote back to say she would love to go out with him. He had the loveliest red hair, which he tried his best to slick back, but because it was curly, it would ping out by the end of the day. Many a Friday night, she had lost herself gazing into his bright blue eyes as he told her great tales of life in the big city of Glasgow.

Friday could not come quickly enough to update Sally all about him and this date offer. What would Sally think? Oh my God, what am I going to wear? Not really being that bothered about what she had worn all these Friday nights collecting fish suppers, it had never entered her head. But this was an actual date. She was excited.

After breakfast the next morning, Moira spoke to Barbara about it.

"What do you think Barbara?"

"I think he is a lovely young man, Moira. You are both adults; just be careful. Remember, the rules in the house are not visiting each other's rooms, we don't want any of those shenanigans under this roof, please!" Barbara waggled a finger at Moira before sitting down.

A proper date! Moira was over the moon, and a bit apprehensive, as to what this could bring.. Brian obviously liked her; she knew that she really liked him. She had enjoyed these past few months of fish and chips with a chat in the evening and the Hi, and Bye stuff in the mornings when she was on an early shift at the cinema.

Worrying her way to work the next day after her chat with Barbara, she was mulling over question after question, What if it all went wrong? What if it changed their relationship and turned out to be a big disaster?

"Get a grip, Moira, she said to herself, you are not fourteen. Just get on with it, if it doesn't work out, what have you lost?"

Friday couldn't come quickly enough to spill out all her concerns to Sally on the phone. There was no way she was telling her dad at this point. Sally's calm voice was just what she needed to put her fears at bay.

"Just treat it like the fish supper evening, it's no different really, Moira."

On her way back to her digs, she realised that their Friday night was off, as Brian had said there would be no point in doing both. He was right, she supposed, but she was feeling the loss of the company tonight. She truly hadn't realised just how close they had become through the Friday night chippy runs.

She had a lovely short, blue skirt with a cream blouse that she had managed to pick up in the week. It looked pretty for a night out. She wondered what to do with her mop of dark curly hair. Put it up or leave it doing its own thing. Decisions, decisions. Trying a couple of up options, she settled on a high ponytail with some curls let loose around her ears.

She could not get to sleep. Imagining all sorts of scenarios for the evening ahead. She thought about what she would do if he tried to hold her hand, or even kiss her. Was she ready for any of that? She knew how she felt about him, so yes, she thought to herself, if he tried to kiss her, she would kiss him back. Then she thought about what if he doesn't try any of that?

The worst thing was that she was working the afternoon shift, finishing at 4.30 pm. They were meeting downstairs at 7.30 pm. She would have to rush home and get ready.

All through the shift, her mind kept drifting off to the evening ahead. Half past four could not come fast enough. Packing up her booth and putting all the cashing up stuff into the office, she made her way home. Nerves were kicking in. Running a hot bubble bath and having a good soak calmed her nerves a bit. Sally's words were ringing in her ears. It was just Friday night on Saturday instead. Opening her room door to Brian's light tap, her nerves disappeared. There he was, smiling broadly at her, in his purple bell-bottoms and blue shirt; he looked so handsome. She was glad she had gone for the blue skirt and cream blouse.

"I thought we were meeting downstairs," she said.

"Barbara and Francis are sitting in the lounge. I wanted us to get away on time."

"Oh, where are we going tonight then?" Moira smiled.

Brian replied, "Just you wait and see."

They walked the short distance to the train station and got a taxi to a swanky new restaurant called Get Stuffed on Park Street. It was busy and friendly. They were seated quickly and served smartly. Moira was disappointed that there were no chips on the menu, and the food was all unfamiliar to her. They chatted while they ate. The conversation flowed just as easily as it did on Friday nights. Leaving the restaurant, they decided to walk home; the evening was mild and still light.

After a few minutes of walking, Brian slipped his hand into hers. Moira felt quite comfortable holding his hand, and they continued to walk laughing and chatting all the way to their digs. Moira could feel the effects of the two glasses of wine mixed with the fresh air.

As they climbed the stairs to her room, she began to feel giddy and excited at the prospect of more happening with this man, whom she had grown so fond of, over the past few months. She opened her room door, and Brian caught her around the waist, pulling her into him. They kissed deeply, and Moira pulled him into the room.

Quietly, Brian asked her, "Are you sure?"

"Yes."

Moira was sure she wanted to know this man more intimately.

It was all over very quickly.

Brian was getting his trousers back on when he asked, "Moira, I hope you are ok with this?"

"Yes, I'm ok, all I'm worried about now is Barbara catching you coming out of my room," she giggled.

At breakfast the next morning, it was very apparent that things had changed between them. Barbara pulled Moira aside after breakfast and asked Moira if she was alright.

"Everything is fine, we had a lovely date last night, and we are now officially a couple."

"Moira, you are so young, are you sure about this?" Barbara asked.

"I'm sure Barbara, I'm talking to my dad tonight about it," Moira replied.

As she walked back upstairs, she thought about it all. Had it all happened too fast? They had been friends for months. Their date had been so comfortable, and they had cemented their attraction by sleeping together. She had no regrets.

Moira could hardly wait till Friday to tell Sally all about it. The week crawled by very slowly; she hadn't seen much of Brian as he had been called away to a job in Manchester. Feeling pangs of worry about falling pregnant. She wondered what she could do about that. Nothing, she would need to hope and pray that she wasn't pregnant.

Brian didn't know about Helen; she didn't feel ready to tell him about her yet. Worried about what he might think of her if he knew. Bobby was coming down to Leeds. Moira was beyond happy. Her dad was aware of the growing relationship between her and Brian; she had been explaining their dates in letters to both Sally and her dad, carefully sending different accounts each week. There were things she was not comfortable telling her dad. There was nothing Sally didn't know. Sally had been down a couple of times in the past couple of months. Moira was happy that Sally and Brian had got on like a house on fire.

Tonight was a special night. Moira's dad was coming to stay the night and come out with her and Brian. She hoped that her dad got on with him. Brian had told her to stop worrying; they would get on just fine.

Feeling nervous, Bobby wondered what Brian would be like. The train wasn't far from Leeds now; Moira would be at the station to meet him. He missed his beautiful girl, but he was glad she was spreading her wings.

Moira could see her dad making his way along the platform.

"Dad, Dad," she was waving furiously, willing him to look up and see her.

He looked up, and their eyes locked. Running to her dad, she threw herself into his arms.

"Ah, Moira, look at you all grown up, woman of the world." Bobby felt tears beginning to pool at the sides of his eyes.

"Dad, are you crying?" Moira was surprised to see a tear roll down her dad's cheek.

"It's just so good to see you," he assured her.

He was fine he assured her, but he had missed her being around so much.

Making their way to the lodgings arm in arm, they chatted the whole way there. Bobby told her funny stories of the events in the village. Nothing much had changed.

Barbara had volunteered to make them some tea that evening, and they could spend time just chatting in the sitting room. After showing her dad around, she left him in his room, telling him that tea would be at 6.30 pm. Barbara was a great cook; she often had workmen staying who paid for both dinner and breakfast.

Barbara served them up some gammon steaks, chips and peas. It was delicious. Moira enjoyed watching her dad and Brian getting to know each other. They looked like they were getting along just fine. It was a great evening together.

Moira had the next day off to spend time with her dad before his 4pm train back home. They had a lovely day exploring Leeds town centre, finding a nice cafe for lunch.

"Are you truly happy, Moira? Do you think Brian is the 'one'?" her dad asked

"Yes, Dad, he is the one; we get on so well. He has a good job too."

"Be very sure, Moira, you don't want to be stuck in a marriage with someone you don't really like after the first love feelings wear off." Bobby knew all about that.

"Don't worry, Dad, I know what I'm doing," Moira assured him.

NINE

WEDDING CHATTER

Watching the train pull away, waving frantically until it was a dot, Moira felt overwhelmed with homesickness. She wanted to run after the train and go home with her dad. *"What's wrong with me?"* she thought to herself. She had been homesick in the early days coming to Leeds, but she hadn't felt it since, until now, watching her dad's train disappear. She was still feeling a bit melancholy when Brian got home that evening.

"What's up, Moira? Are you missing your dad?"

"I am feeling a bit homesick. I felt so sad watching his train leave," Moira replied.

"Right turn that frown upside down, let's plan a visit to see him next month, yes, let's do that, Moira, I would love to see where you come from," Brian said.

"That would be brilliant. Let's book our time off work tomorrow." Moira said with excitement.

The month had rolled on uneventfully, and they were on the train to Dumfries. Moira was excited to show Brian where she lived. They were going to get the bus from Dumfries to her village when Moira heard her name being called.

"Woo hoo, Moira, over here!" Sally was shouting and waving at them.

Her mum had brought the car down to pick them up as a surprise. It was hugs all round.

They were staying the whole weekend and travelling back on Monday. Moira felt so at home in her house again. She did miss village life, but she knew she was not going to be coming back to live here. They had a great weekend, including Sally in most of their plans. Sally and Brian got on so well, he seemed to win everybody over.

It was Sunday evening, and Brian asked her if she would like to go for a walk.

"That would be lovely, let's head up the hill to the woods," Moira decided.

Reaching the top of the hill, they turned round and admired the view.

Brain turned to her, saying, "What made you leave this beautiful place, Moira?"

Looking up at him, she sighed and said wistfully, "I know it is idyllic, but I needed more,"

Wrapping his arms around her, he kissed her passionately. "I love you, Moira."

Kneeling, he took her hand in his and asked her to marry him.

"I love you too, Brian Morrison, and, yes, I will marry you, any day you like."

Pulling him up, they kissed again. Heading into the woods, they found a quiet spot and consummated the proposal.

Bobby was delighted to hear about the proposal. His little girl was going to be a wife. They had said they would be going to the church in the morning to set a date. They didn't need to wait for ages; they knew how they felt about each other.

The minister was happy to see them. They set a date for September 20th, which was three months away. Walking through the village to tell Sally, on the way there, they bumped into Fiona and Gavin Barnes.

"Moira, how are you? Who is this handsome chap?" Fiona asked.

Smiling at her friend, she said, "This is my fiancé Brian, we are getting married here in September, and you two are invited."

"How wonderful, Moira, all the very best."

Gavin leaned forward and gave Brian a hearty farmer's handshake.

"They seem nice, Moira. Who are they?" Brian asked.

Moira almost blurted out that Fiona had been the one she had left Helen with.

"They are our neighbours from the farm you could see from the top of the hill," Moira answered.

Reaching Sally's house, Moira ran into the kitchen; she couldn't wait to tell Sally the news. "Wow, Moira, that's amazing," said Sally.

Looking intently at her friend, she asked Moira, "Are you sure about such a big commitment?"

"Yes, I love him dearly. We have been together for a long time now. It is the natural next step, and I am so looking forward to it. Will you be my bridesmaid?"

"Of course I will, you goose, you don't have to ask me twice," Sally said, laughing.

Staying for a quick cup of tea, they chatted about the big day. As they said their goodbyes, it was hugs all round.

Their journey back to Leeds was full of wedding chatter. Brian rolled his eyes a few times at Moira's long lists of things to do. Looking at his wife to be, her cheeks were glowing, her hair was shining, full dark curls bouncing around as she talked about their plans. She would make a great wife. He kissed her to get a quick break from the constant wedding chatter.

TEN

THE WEDDING

It was already mid-August. The wedding plans were going well. It was going to be a small affair. Immediate family and friends only. Brian had no siblings or parents to invite, but he had an aunt and uncle with their children, who were close to him, coming to the wedding.

Moira had chosen a pretty long cream dress to wear for her big day. She was aware that white wasn't what she wanted to wear. It felt a bit wrong considering everything that had happened.

They had both taken two weeks off work for the wedding. Moira was awake early as usual when she heard a tap on her bedroom door. Assuming it was Brian, she opened the door with a smile. It was Barbara.

"There is a phone call for you, Moira."

Moira's heart leapt in her chest; something was wrong. Why would she be getting a phone call? Barbara only allowed calls through that were an emergency.

"Hello," said Moira tentatively.

"Moira, it's Patsy. I think you will need to come home, dear. Your dad was taken into the hospital late last night. I hadn't seen him for a couple of days. I went up to the house, and he was lying in the living room chair. I couldn't get any sense out of him, so I called Dr Ottiwell, and he called an ambulance."

"What's happened to him?"

Moira was already crying. Barbara put her arm around her and took the phone. Moira was sobbing loudly.

"I will get her on the train to Dumfries, Patsy."

Barbara put the phone down and held on to Moira till she calmed down.

"Come on, Moira, you need to get ready and go be with your dad, love."

Moira packed a bag in a haze of tears.

"What about Brian? Will you let him know where I am?" Moira asked Barbara.

"Don't you worry about him, I will let him know what's happened when he gets back from Glasgow," Barbara said.

The journey to Dumfries felt like it took forever; her mind was racing, alongside her heart. What on earth had happened to her dad? Patsy was waiting for her outside the hospital main entrance, where they had agreed to meet.

"Moira, your dad is in a bad way. The doctors are not sure what has happened. They think it is his heart, but they are waiting for some tests to come back," Patsy said, looking worried.

Rushing along the bleak hospital corridors, Moira felt surge after surge of hot tears falling down her face. Reaching the ward, Patsy gave her a hanky to dry her eyes before she went in.

Bobby was lying motionless, his breathing was laboured and noisy.

"Dad, it's Moira. I love you so much; you have to get better."

Moira saw his eyelids flicker; he had heard her voice.

She leaned over to kiss him gently on the cheek, whispering in his ear, "Dad, please don't leave me alone," then feeling a sliver of guilt for being so selfish.

Moira held her dad's hand for what seemed like an eternity, just listening to his crackling breaths. The doctor had been in and explained that there was nothing they could do for him. He had had a brain bleed; it was just a matter of time. Whatever time he had left, Moira was determined he would not spend a second of it alone. At 1.15 am, her beloved father drew his last breath. Patsy, her husband Jack and Brian were all there too.

"Let's get you home, Moira. Your dad has gone, you need to let him go." Brian took her arm to lead her out of the room.

"No, I don't want to leave him." The tears would not stop flowing as she held on to his hand.

Giving her a few more minutes, he gently tried to move her out of the room.

"It is time to go, Moira," Patsy said quietly.

Arriving back at the house and looking around, nothing, absolutely nothing had changed in the house. It was all just as she remembered it as a child growing up until she had left. It was now her house. She had so much to think about. The next morning, Sally came bursting through the door, almost knocking her to the floor in a big, tearful bearhug.

"Oh, Moira, I'm so, so sorry, but I'm so happy to see you, I've missed you so much."

Stepping back from her friend, Moira could not believe her eyes. Sally had a little baby bump!

"Oh my God, Sally, are you pregnant?" Moira gasped.

"I know, I know, I'm so sorry I couldn't tell you. Mum made me swear not to say anything. I really wanted to tell you when you were up in July."

Plopping herself down in one of the kitchen chairs, Moira rubbed her forehead in disbelief.

What was going on it was one shock after another. Putting the kettle on, Moira demanded to know everything that had been going on. Sally had gone out with one of the boys from a neighbouring village. They had been quite serious, but when he found out she was pregnant, he wanted nothing to do with Sally or the baby.

Sally's mum was going to bring up the baby, allowing Sally to go to college and have a career. Moira was annoyed by how easy it seemed for Sally to be pregnant and get the support from her mum. Moira had to remind herself that Sally wasn't fifteen, was she?

Allowing her mind to wander back to that cold night in the woods when little Helen had arrived, she started to cry again. Comforting her best friend, Sally had no idea that it had nothing to do with her dad dying, that she was crying. Moira had her secrets.

Sally had decided to stay at Moira's until the funeral, which gave Moira some much-needed company and Sally some breathing space from her mum. The week went by in a blur; well-wishers had dropped off cooked food and cards expressing their sympathy. Her dad was well known and liked in the village. He had been a steady, mild-mannered man. She was so grateful to everyone who had helped her get everything ready for the funeral.

Brian was on his way back up to be with her for the funeral and to stay for a few days. Moira had given her notice at the cinema and at her lodgings. She knew she wouldn't be going back to Leeds. Much as she had enjoyed the experience, she knew that she would need time to get over the fact that she was now entirely on her own. Even though she was doing fine on her own in Leeds, she had always had her dad there if anything had gone wrong.

After the funeral, she still had a wedding to prepare for.

ELEVEN

A NEW ADVENTURE

A new adventure awaited her: marriage to Brian. Waiting at the village bus stop, she felt little butterflies in her tummy as the bus trundled towards the stop. Brian stepped off the bus into Moira's waiting embrace. She was so happy to see him. Absence really had made the heart fonder. Knowing, in that moment, that she loved him with all her heart made her feel safe and secure. His tall, slim frame and her small, curvy frame made for an odd-looking couple.

Hardly believing that he was here, Moira stared up at him, searching his face and his eyes, looking for and finding all that was familiar to her. She felt happy and ready for their upcoming wedding resting in his arms. Hand in hand, they made their way up to Moira's house. He was going to stay for the funeral. Then they would make the trip back down to collect their things from Barbara's lodgings.

Reaching the house, she let him know that Sally had gone back to her mum. They had the place to themselves. The door had hardly shut when Brian swooped her up into a huge embrace, kissing her as if they had been apart for years. He had missed her, and she had missed him, too. She needed some comfort. Leading him to the stairs, he followed her up to the bedroom.

Knowing full well that the village would be talking about Moira having a man staying with her, she didn't really care; they were getting married a few weeks after the funeral anyway.

The day of the funeral dawned bright with a slight breeze. Grateful to have a good friend in Sally, and Sally's mum, by her side at the funeral; she knew she wouldn't have coped without them. It was hard to lean on Brian; he had only met her dad that one time. She could see he was struggling with all the well-wishers and subtle questions about who he was. He was quick to tell them he was Moira's fiancé.

As the well-wishers filed past, some hugging her, some shaking her hand and sharing their condolences, she noticed Fiona Barnes making her way up the line. They had shared grief over the loss of little Helen. As they locked eyes, both women cried as they hugged.

"Please come to the house after," Moira said as they embraced.

Fiona said she couldn't as Gavin needed her on the farm. She promised to pop over sometime that week.

Taking Moira's arm, Sally's mum guided her out of the church towards the burial plot. Seeing Fiona had brought the tears that she had stoically held back throughout the funeral service. Putting an arm around her waist, Brian whispered in her ear.

"You will be fine, it's okay to cry, you've just lost your dad."

Pulling her close to him before letting her go, she smiled up at him through the tears, thanking him for being here for her.

Watching as the pallbearers lowered the coffin into the plot beside her mother was unbearable. Moira's chest was so tight with emotion that she was sure her heart might burst. It was striking home hard that she was entirely on her own. Her mum had been an only child, and her dad had a brother whom she had only seen twice, the second time was today. He seemed a bit distant. She didn't think she would see him again.

Inviting only close friends and family back to the house, she made her way slowly down the hill. Two of her mum's church friends had been making sandwiches and cake for those coming back with her. Walking through the front door, she made her way to the kitchen, where a wonderful spread was laid out on the big kitchen table, with big kettles on the stove for hot drinks.

Sally was doing a grand job of herding people into the living room, giving her the time to step out into the back garden to release some of the pent-up emotion of the day. Her heart was aching; she felt the loss like losing a limb.

Stepping back into the kitchen, taking a deep breath, she smiled at Valerie as she busied herself taking plates of food into the living room for the guests. Valerie and Emily had been such a help; she was so grateful they had stepped in to do all the food and serving. They really were good at this kind of thing.

Her dad's brother Richard made a beeline towards her as soon as she stepped into the living room. He had come on his own, stating that his wife was ill.

"I'm so sorry, Moira. I can't stay long, and it's a three-hour drive home."

She wished him well, thanking him for coming as she waved him off on his way. *"Well, that was awkward,"* she thought to herself. Not one question about how she was going to cope, he must know he is the only relative I have. Dwelling on his lack of compassion was not going to help her move through this day and the years to come; that was for sure.

Getting through the small talk was tough, and listening to stories about her dad was tough. She had to make her way through the afternoon, wishing she could be somewhere else.

Eventually, she managed to prise old Mrs Stuart out of her dad's chair towards the front door. Full of stories of the past, she was entertaining, but really needed to be on her way. Thanking her for coming and promising to visit soon, Moira slid down the back of the door as she closed it. The tears came and would not stop.

Patsy found her there a couple of minutes later. Sitting on the floor beside her, she pulled her close with an arm around her shoulders and told her to stay and cry as long as she needed to. Brian popped his head out of the kitchen, where he had been helping clear up. Patsy waved him away. Shutting the door, he went back to helping make Val, Emily and Sally laugh with his silly stories.

Sally and Brian were enjoying a warm whisky together in a spotlessly clean kitchen when Patsy came in.

"Moira is in her bed, asleep. She needs to rest. She's always been the strong one. Always being there for others. It's time for her to be looked after. I'm so glad you are here, Brian. She adores you and needs you more than ever now."

"Come on, you, it's time we left."

Throwing her eyes at Sally, Patsy waved her out the back door.

TWELVE

THE FUTURE

Waking up to the familiar sounds of home, Moira stretched out in her bed. She wondered where Brian had gone. Swinging her legs out of bed, looking at the clock, she was horrified to see it was after twelve. Slipping her dressing gown on, she headed downstairs. She could smell bacon, her tummy rumbled, and, realising she hadn't eaten much the day before, she now felt very hungry. Patsy was in the kitchen frying bacon, eggs and sausages.

"Nice to see you up and about, Moira."

Sally popped her head in the back door, "We are out here, Moira."

She had been outside smoking and chatting with Brian. Hugging her friend, Moira sat down at the table. Sally went back out to finish her cigarette with Brian.

"What's going to be next for me, Patsy?"

"What is it you want to do, Moira? Stay here? Or sell up and move? And more importantly, what is going on with you and Brian? What does he want to do?" Patsy asked.

Not really knowing what the answer was to any of the questions, Moira called Brian and Sally in to eat breakfast.

It was great having a bit of company for a while. Eventually, they left. Patsy said she had left the next two days' dinners in the fridge; they just needed to be warmed through.

"I fancy going for a walk, do you want to come with me?"

Brian looked up from the paper and agreed that a walk was a good idea.

Heading away from the village, they wandered up the hill towards the woods. Holding hands, they walked quietly for a while. Knowing they had plans to make, Brian broke the silence by asking Moira if she intended to stay here. He hoped not. The silence of the country-side was starting to close in on him. He was used to city life.

Unsure of how to answer him, she remained silent. Thoughts were rushing through her head at breakneck speed. She wanted a moment to think before blurting out anything too emotional. They were just about to pass the spot where she had given birth to Helen. The memory of that cold night came rushing back as if it had been yester-day. He knew nothing about her secret. How do you start to tell someone you love something like that? She knew that now was not the right time.

"Can we wait until tomorrow to talk about our plans? It has to be our plans, not my plans, or your plans, Brian. Let's sleep on it and talk it through tomorrow."

As they walked back to the house, Moira asked him to make his way back on his own; she wanted to call in on Fiona Barnes. They had forged a bond through the death of Moira's baby. Fiona had taken in the baby and renamed her Alice. When Alice had died, Moira had confessed that it was her baby that she had left on the doorstep that night.

Knocking on the farm door, standing on the very step she had laid Helen, knowing that Fiona would be the perfect parent, she felt huge emotions welling up in her chest. She had a good bond with Fiona. Her husband Gavin never knew the baby belonged to Moira.

Opening the door, Fiona was surprised to see Moira there.

"Come away in," Fiona said with a smile.

Bursting into tears, Moira stepped into the hallway. Fiona scooped her into her arms and led her into the living room.

"I'm sorry, Fiona, I shouldn't have come, I had to come and see you," Moira said through her tears.

Smiling at Moira, she replied, "Things are just fine, Moira, Gavin, and I are expecting our first child in around five months."

Moira's heart soared, "That news has just made a very sad time seem more bearable. Thanks for telling me."

They chatted a while till there wasn't much else to say. Moira felt a sense of peace knowing that this couple were being blessed with the child they had always longed for. As Moira made her way home, she stopped to breathe, she looked around at all the space, the familiar trees, the sounds she had heard since she was a baby. The church spire was poking up into the sky as it always had. The path she had walked every day as a child. The exact path she had walked down after leaving Helen at the farm. So many memories came flooding back. She felt happy here, comfortable here. But she knew that Brian wasn't really feeling the confines of village life.

After a few minutes enjoying the scenes around her, she made her way home. The smell of something burning greeted her as she made her way towards the open back door. Dashing into the kitchen, there was Brian busily burning their tea on the stove.

"Not going to be letting you do the cooking when we are married, then," she laughed.

The new day dawned bright and sunny. Waking up feeling refreshed for the first time in a week, Moira skipped downstairs to get breakfast started. Looking around the kitchen, she felt a wave of emotion. This whole house was now hers. She had received a letter from the solicitors in Dumfries telling her to make an appointment at her earliest convenience. The letter sounded rather grand and a little scary at the same time.

She would call them after breakfast to make the appointment. Sorting out a tray to take up to Brian, she noticed a piece of paper hanging down from the drawer above the cupboard. She pulled it out, and it was a brown envelope with her mum's name handwritten on the front. Popping it back in the drawer, she realised that this was another big job she would need to do. Sorting out all the things that belonged to her parents.

The very thought of going through their things was choking her with sadness, and going into cupboards and drawers that had been strictly off-limits as a child was going to feel weird.

Brian was heading back to Leeds in two days. The week had flown by, and she didn't want him to go, but she knew that he had to get back to work. She knew she had to stay here for the time being to sort out the house and everything else. They had agreed that today they would sit down and try to work out their plans for the future.

When she called the solicitors in Dumfries to make an appointment, she was asked if she could make it later that afternoon. It was a bit sooner than she felt ready for, but saying yes, she knew it was better to get this out of the way. She was also happy that Brian could come with her.

Deciding to have their chat and tea at the *Globe* on the sands made it feel more like a nice day out. Choosing a lovely lemon dress to wear, with some smart white shoes. She wondered if her outfit was appropriate to go to the solicitors, should she be wearing something staider - a suit or something? Sticking with the dress, she added a lemon bag to the ensemble.

Patsy arrived in the car to take them both to Dumfries. There were only two buses in and two buses out of the village daily, except on Sundays.

"Is Sally not coming in?" Moira asked.

"No, not today, I have some work for her to do at home," said Patsy as they set off on their twenty-two-mile journey into the town.

Parking her car at the sands, Patsy waved them off as she went off to do some shopping and meet her friends for tea later on. Moira was starting to feel very nervous about what would be said at the solicitors.

Heading into the big building and up the stairs to Mr Grey's office, Moira's heart was beating so hard she felt sure the lady leading them up the stairs could hear it.

Standing up straight away as they walked in, the solicitor introduced himself as Sandy Grey. He was an elderly man; he looked like he should have retired many years ago.

"I knew your mother at school, Moira, take a seat, my dear," he said, waving at two chairs on the opposite side of his desk.

"My condolences on the loss of your father recently, which sadly brings you in to see me today," Sandy smiled at Moira.

Bringing two folders out of his drawer, he coughed almost ceremoniously as he opened the first one.

"You may not be surprised to learn that the house and the land around it have been left to you, Moira."

Sandy looked up, waiting for an acknowledgement that she understood.

"Yes, I do understand that, thank you," she answered.

The second folder seemed to contain more. Coughing again, Sandy told her she had inherited just over seven thousand pounds along with the house.

"What? How can that be possible?" Moira asked.

Looking at Brian, she said, "I had no idea they had all that money." Her heart was beating at a hundred miles an hour now.

Looking directly at Moira again, Sandy said, "What I am about to tell you may come as a bit of a shock."

Sandy went on to explain that the money she had just inherited had been given to her mum as a goodwill gesture for taking in a wealthy landowner's grandchild.

Mr Grey went on to say that Moira's mum, Joy, had been a housekeeper for the family. The wife had fallen pregnant while her husband was away for a year in America.

As it slowly dawned on Moira that she was that child, it felt as if her heart had stopped for a moment. *"How could that be?"* she thought.

She looked at Brian, he had no idea what to say to his wife to be.

Asking a few questions, Moira grew frustrated with Sandy's lack of answers.

The rest of the meeting went by in a blur; Moira had no idea what else had been said.

Brian helped her up as Sandy stood, extending his hand, saying, "Please don't hesitate to call me if you have any more questions, Moira."

Questions! Of course, she had bloody questions. But probably not ones that Sandy Grey could answer.

Out on the street in the bright sunshine, she could feel Brian giving her a little shake.

"Are you ok, Moira?"

He sounded concerned.

"Of course I'm not ok," she snapped.

The concrete pavement felt like marshmallows. She desperately wanted to scream.

"I'm not Moira Kirkwell," kept running through her brain.

"Who am I then?"

"How did this happen?"

"Where are my real parents?"

The questions kept building up in her brain like a massive traffic jam. There was nowhere for the thoughts to go. She had none of the answers, and the only two people who did have the answers were dead.

Putting an arm around her waist, Brian began to guide Moira towards the Globe. She needed to eat and a stiff drink. Sitting a dazed Moira down, he ordered a whisky for her and a pint for himself. She was in some shock. He wasn't too sure how he was going to manage this. He was glaringly aware that he was about to marry a very wealthy young woman, though.

Gratefully throwing the straight whisky down her neck, Moira asked for another one and a hot, sweet cup of tea. The whisky slowed the myriad of questions, and the tea helped her return to reality.

"What on earth has just happened?" she sighed.

"I'm not their daughter. But I am their daughter. I'm two people at the same time."

Her mind was in turmoil, her heart felt broken and betrayed.

Brain looked at her strained expression with compassion. What a shock to be told that your parents were not your parents.

"Maybe you should try to eat something," he said.

Picking up the menu, Moira ordered her favourite haggis, neeps and tatties. Nowhere made it better than here at the Globe.

The food arrived quickly, and the smell of the meal made Moira realise just how hungry she was.

"Moira, I know you have had a shock, but I have to go back to Leeds on Friday. We only really have tomorrow together to talk about what we are going to do. I truly want you to marry me, still, Moira," he blurted out.

Moira looked at him in surprise, "Why would I not want to marry you now?"

"We can chat tonight when we get home, Brian," she said, wondering what had made him think she wouldn't want to marry him now.

As arranged, Patsy came into the Globe at 8.30 pm to take them home.

"Moira has had a bit of a shock," Brian said.

"What's happened, Moira?"

Patsy took her hand as she sat at the table beside them.

"Oh, Patsy, my mum and dad are not mine, I'm someone else's child, did you know about this?"

"No, Moira, not at all. I can't think why this could be, you look so much like your dad," said Patsy.

"Let's get you two home, and we can talk about it all in the car."

Patsy was aware of other diners looking at them as Moira began to cry.

The drive home felt awkward. Patsy wasn't sure what to say. Moira was quiet in the back of the car. Brian chatted about nothing interesting in the front seat.

Arriving outside Moira's house, Patsy asked Moira if she wanted her to come in.

"No, we will be fine, thank you, Patsy. We can chat tomorrow."

Kicking off her shoes and feeling the throb of her feet was the first real thing she had felt since being at the solicitors. She was glad they had eaten. Cooking was the last thing on her mind right now.

"Moira, come and sit down, you look awful," said Brian.

"Thanks for that. Can you pour me a drink, please, Brian? I'm really struggling to get my head round this."

"Of course," filling a glass with whisky and lemonade, he put it down on the coffee table and sat down beside her on the couch.

"What can I do to help you, Moira?"

With tears filling her eyes, she said, "Just hold me."

Wrapping his arms around her, they sat like that for a while, until Moira looked up at him. They began to kiss gently. Lying in each other's arms after making love. Moira asked Brian if he would help her find out who she was.

"Of course, I will, Moira, whatever you need me to do to help, I will do it."

They spent the rest of the evening talking about their plans and how on earth Moira could find out more about who she was.

82

Thirteen

Heather

Waving Brian off on the bus felt very sad, they had put their banns in at the village church, they would be married in six weeks. Brian was heading back to Leeds to sort out all their things. He had an aunt and uncle in Glasgow, that he wanted to see and invite to the wedding.

She would miss him, but she needed the space to think and work out what she would do. The house was full of her parents' things. She wanted to sort through everything. Maybe she would find some clues about what had gone on around her birth.

Moira started clearing out the kitchen drawers; two of them were full of letters and papers. It was emotional to read the things that had been sent to her parents. She came across a familiar-looking brown envelope with her mother's name on the front. She remembered seeing it around the time of her dad's funeral.

Opening the letter, she saw a second envelope inside with her name on it. Putting the first letter down, she opened the one addressed to her.

Dearest Moira,

I do hope it is you reading this. You are my granddaughter. My daughter Margaret gave birth to you. You were the tiniest little mite when you were born. You had a shock of dark curly hair.

Margaret could not keep you considering the circumstances. We decided it was best for you to come live with your father and Joy. I know that this must be a shock to you.

As a thank you to your father for agreeing never to see Margaret again and terminating their employment to bring you up, we put some money into a trust for you to be given to you upon the deaths of both your parents or when you reached the age of twenty-one.

I want to wish you well in the future and apologise for this situation. This should never have happened.

Your grandmother
Heather.

"Unbelievable," shouted Moira to the kitchen as she sat on the nearest kitchen chair.

Tears streamed down her cheeks, "How could you have lied to me all of my life?" she said to the letter.

The story just got wilder. One minute she was nobody's child, the next minute it looked like she was her dad's love child!

"Oh my god, this is just awful," she said angrily.

Moving through to the living room, she poured herself a drink and called Sally.

"I'm on my way up, Moira," said Sally.

"I just can't believe all this, Sally," said Moira as her friend came in the back door.

"I'm so bloody angry, how could they not even tell me?" fumed Moira.

"Think about it, how could they tell you, what would you have thought?" said Sally, draping her arm around Moira's shoulders.

"No wonder my mum always looked unhappy, now I know why she was always angry at everyone," Moira said, feeling sorry for her mum.

The two friends chatted for a while, but didn't really reach any conclusions about the situation. Except that Moira was hurt and confused by these revelations.

"Moira, do you want me to help you tidy out the rest of the drawers, in case anything else comes to light?" Sally asked.

"That would be great, Sally, at least I will have you here with me if we uncover any more secret children," Moira said, trying to make light of the whole thing.

Nothing else of any genuine interest came out of the kitchen drawers. They moved upstairs to her parents' bedroom. In the big chest of drawers, it was all just clothes. Her dad had not sorted out Joy's things. There were bags and bags of clothes building up by the time they had cleared out all the drawers.

Kneeling to go through the drawers at each side of the bed. Moira had her dad's side, and Sally was doing Joy's side.

Sally looked over at Moira after a few minutes, seeing her friend with a small red notebook in her hands and tears quietly streaming down her face.

She asked, "Moira, are you ok? What have you found?"

Motioning Sally to come round, she handed the book to her.

"Wow, Moira, your dad has written some beautiful poems." Sally's eyes widened as she read some of them.

"I can't believe it, who knew he was so talented?" Moira said, knowing this book would never leave her side again.

Finishing up for the night, Sally offered to stay over and help again in the morning.

The next day started off raining heavily, and Patsy joined them to help sort out her parents' stuff. Moira showed her the letter she had found and the book of poetry that her dad had written.

"Oh, my, your dad was such a talented writer. I knew he could write; he had a job before you came along at the Standard newspaper. He wrote a couple of short stories in it."

Patsy looked wistful as she remembered the stories.

"I wonder if we can get back copies of them," Patsy said.

Moira asked, "Do you know where else he worked before I was born?"

"Gosh, he had a few jobs, he worked at the farriers at Gretna for a bit, I remember he had a job at some stables, your mum worked at the big house there too."

Patsy couldn't think of any more jobs before Moira had appeared.

Moira knew that her search would have to start by finding out who lived at the big house and exactly where the big house was. She had a wedding to sort out before that.

"Let's concentrate on my wedding plans. I can look for whoever Margaret is after that," Moira said more cheerily than she felt.

<h1 style="text-align:center">FOURTEEN</h1>

<h1 style="text-align:center">MRS MORRISON</h1>

Her dress arrived two weeks before the big day a stunning, flouncy cream full length dress with a V neck and fitted waist. It fitted her perfectly.

Brian was arriving back in the village in four days. It felt like an eternity that he had been away. He was bringing his Aunt and Uncle with him. They were going to stay in a holiday cottage that Moira had booked for them until the day after the wedding.

Watching Brian making his way along the lane in the little brown car he had bought, her heart felt fit to burst. She knew she loved him with all of her heart.

Her face beaming, she ran out to meet him.

The day of the wedding dawned grey and drizzly. *"Great,"* thought Moira, *"this monstrosity of a dress is going to get all mucky."* It wasn't far enough away from the house to warrant getting in and out of a car. Sally had engaged two brolly holders to walk the short distance to the church with them.

Walking into the church and seeing Brian looking so handsome in his kilt and shirt with a tartan plaid across his shoulder. He was beaming at her as she made her way down towards him. She had asked to come down the aisle to one of her dad's poems that she had found. It made her feel like he was with her.

The day went by in a blur of excitement. The meal was simple but set out so nicely in the church hall. There were toasts aplenty. They nipped home for an hour after the photos to change for the evening ceilidh. Feeling a bit tipsy, Moira flopped down on the sofa.

"I almost wish we didn't need to go tonight," she giggled.

"You are a funny little thing, Moira," said Brian as he tipped her chin for a kiss. "Welcome home, Mrs Morrison."

They danced the night away. Making sure they connected with all of their guests. Thankfully, they didn't have far to go home.

Lifting her head off the pillow the next morning was no small task. Moira felt like she had been hit by a train. Head pounding, she made her way downstairs, leaving Brian snoring, to find some Anadin. Coffee in hand, she went to sit on the back doorstep. With no desire to eat or to cook, she decided to stay on the step and mull over the day before. She was now Mrs Moira Morrison. It sounded like a teacher's name. She could train to be a teacher. She wasn't really sure what she wanted to do going forward.

They hadn't really made any final decisions on where they were going to live. Glasgow might be the best option. They were renting a little cottage for a week to have their honeymoon.

Once the Anadin and coffee had worked their magic, she set about making her husband's breakfast.

She was excited about the future they had together. They had talked about children. She would love to start a family, she had said, and Brian had readily agreed. Knowing they didn't need to save for a flat or baby things, nothing was stopping them from having children straight away.

There had been heated arguments about selling her house and using the money, alongside her 'inheritance', to buy a house, but Moira didn't want to do that. Losing her identity had been an enormous blow; losing her childhood home? She wasn't ready for that. No matter how often Patsy assured her that her mum and dad were her parents, as she had never known anything else since the day she was born, she still had this big hole in her heart. She knew she would need to track down the person who had actually given birth to her. She often wondered if they ever thought about her.

All she had managed to find out was that there had been a big house on the other side of the loch. It had burned to the ground around seventeen years ago. No one seemed to know much about the family that had lived there, or where they had gone.

Deciding to move to Glasgow hadn't been that difficult; there were plenty of work opportunities. Moving away would be hard, but they needed a fresh start. Brian just wasn't a country lover. Someone would snap up the chance to rent the house, and Sally had agreed to help out, keeping an eye on any tenants.

Sally had been her best friend since they were children. It had been great being home and having her confidant to talk to again. It wouldn't be long until Sally would be a mother. Sally had told her that the baby was now going to be put up for adoption. Moira had been surprised; she had thought Patsy would help her look after the baby.

Sally had been so upset telling Moira about the baby being put up for adoption. She had told Moira that she might run away to keep the baby. Moira was a bit worried about her.

Knowing her own thoughts on how she felt not knowing now, where she had come from, the news had stabbed her in the heart. Moira and Brian had packed; it was time to say goodbye to Glendoon. As Brian filled the car, she looked around one last time. Memories of laughter with her dad. Her mum roaring at her to get dressed and get downstairs, 'or else' made her smile. Sunday's memories were of being dragged to church for the Sunday service. It was hard to believe she was twenty, married and moving to Glasgow.

Sally and Patsy were making their way up the lane to the house. She would miss them both. Patsy had taken on the role of mother of the bride at her wedding. She had been a tower of strength to her throughout everything. Sometimes she wished she could tell her about Helen.

She smiled to herself as she looked around, she was happy to know Fiona and Gavin were going to have their own child.

"What are you smiling about, Mrs Morrison?" Brian said with a cheeky grin on his own face.

He was glad Moira had agreed to move to Glasgow. The countryside was lovely, but it just wasn't him. He was delighted they had the money to rent themselves a flat on Copeland Road in Ibrox. They were nice spacious tenement flats.

Turning round, he saw Sally and Patsy making their way up the path to say their goodbyes. Patsy had been a great source of strength for Moira. Sally was so different to Moira, tall, blonde and frivolous. At the same time, Moira was dark, dainty and a bit more serious. Something had changed in Moira since she had received the news about where she had come from; it seemed she was happy that she might be her dad's child, but sad that her mum had had to endure whatever had happened to her nature for taking in Moira.

"Oh, you two, have the best time. I will be down to visit as soon as this little bump has gone."

Moira was surprised at how easily Sally had said that.

"You are always going to be welcome, Sally."

Moira would miss her friend, but they were near enough for her to visit often.

Giving Sally and Patsy a big hug, Brian took the last bag to the car and got in. He wanted to let them say their emotional goodbyes without him. He didn't really have that level of connection with them. They were Moira's friends.

After a few minutes, he beeped the car horn to get Moira in the car. They had an appointment to pick up the keys and sign the tenancy agreement at three o'clock. He wanted to get moving.

With lots of waving and promises to phone once they got there, finally, they drove off down the lane and through the village. Brian breathed an inward sigh of relief while Moira dabbed her eyes.

They arrived at half past two outside the tenement. The street was busy. There was a little paper shop at the bottom of the street, which would be handy, thought Moira.

With the keys in hand and the paperwork all signed. Brian took Moira's hand just outside the door.

"What are you doing, Brian?"

Swooping her up into his arms, he carried her over the threshold of their first home.

They had a great couple of weeks exploring where they lived and making the flat more homely. There were plenty of shops on the main road, and Govan market wasn't far away either.

Brian had found a new job at the big football stadium nearby, and Moira was starting her new job on Monday, doing filing at nearby offices on Paisley Road West. Her tummy was turning with nerves. Monday dawned with a heavy mist. Looking out the window, she was dismayed as her curls would frizz up while walking to work in that. Her stomach was churning with nerves. Breakfast was a struggle; she kept feeling sick.

The worry was all for nothing. The women at the offices were all lovely. They were happy to welcome her onto the team. Giving her the job of answering the telephones, as she had what they were calling a 'posh' voice.

They settled into their new life together. Moira enjoyed being a wife. Brian seemed to be happy in his new job. He got to watch the games on Saturdays, which was a bonus.

They had a phone installed, and it was great being able to call Sally on Fridays and get all the news. Fiona Barnes had had a little boy; they had called him Martin. Sally had given birth to a little boy. She had called him Steven. She had only held him for a day before he had to go to his new family.

It was a tough time all round. Moira had told Sally to come down the following weekend to stay with them and take her mind off what had happened. She knew how she might be feeling.

Moira had her own news. She knew she was pregnant. Thinking back to when she found out she was carrying Helen, she recognised the feelings now that she had time to think. Morning sickness had been mild, luckily for her. She had been to the doctors and was, in fact, pregnant.

Waiting for Brian to come home that evening, she had made a steak pie with potatoes and veg. Coming into the warm kitchen, he could smell the dinner.

"What's all this, steak pie on a Tuesday?"

"Sit down, Mr Morrison, I have some news for you," she ruffled his hair on the way to her seat.

"What is it?" he asked, raising his eyebrows. "What's going on, Moira?"

"Two things, actually. Sally is coming to stay this weekend, and we are going to have a baby."

Moira looked at him to see his response.

"A baby!" he shouted almost choking on a potato.

"Yes, and don't even think about saying, how did that happen," she smiled at him, waiting for his approval.

"Wow, Moira, that was quick, I didn't think it would be so soon."

It wasn't the overjoyed, rushing over to hug her reaction she was hoping for.

"Are you happy about it?" Moira asked, worried that it might be too soon.

"Of course I am, I'm just surprised, I can't believe I'm going to be a dad."

FIFTEEN

DANIEL

Moira was all booked in for a scan. Brian had the morning off to come with her.

From the scan, they were able to tell her that she was around eighteen weeks pregnant. They looked at each other in surprise. Moira was excited and looking forward to enjoying the rest of the pregnancy, knowing that she didn't need to hide it this time.

She phoned Sally to tell her the good news before she came down. She had given birth to a little boy a month earlier. She had decided to put him up for adoption. Well, as Sally put it, her parents had made that decision. Moira didn't understand why. But, she knew Sally was starting University in September.

Sally had told Moira that her parents had said having a career was more important. She would have been quite happy being a single mum.

Sally sat on the train to Glasgow, feeling washed out and miserable. She missed her little boy. She had whispered in his ear that, one day she would come and find him. She told him over and over that she loved him. The gut-wrenching feeling as the nurse prised him out of her arms was something that she would never forget.

She had cried for days after it. University seemed a poor prize for losing her baby. She didn't even want to go now. She was looking forward to seeing Moira and Brian.

Brian picked her up from Glasgow Central Station. Brian said that Moira wasn't feeling too great. They had a great chat on the way back to the flat.

It had been a great weekend, but Sally had drunk far too much. Pouring out all her frustrations around the loss of her baby, Steven. Moira had gone to bed early, leaving poor Brian to listen to it all. She would comfort her friend in the morning. She had planned a nice shopping trip for them both to cheer her up. It was heartbreaking listening to Sally's feelings about having to give up her little boy.

Baby Daniel was born on the 6th of March 1971. He screamed his way into the world in the Southern General maternity ward after a two-day labour. Helen's birth had been so starkly different. Cold, dark and in as much silence as Moira could manage, she had arrived quickly and quietly into the world.

After a week in the hospital, they were finally allowed to take Daniel home. He was a noisy little boy. It felt like he cried all the time. He struggled to feed and sleep. They were permanently exhausted. Brian had dark circles around his eyes. The flat suddenly filled with baby stuff and noise. Trying and failing to feed Daniel herself, Moira had moved on to bottles and formula. It did the trick, helping him sleep a bit longer.

She was exhausted. Volunteering to do all the night feeds, as Brian was still working long hours. Sitting quietly one night watching Daniel feed, she looked down at his soft face and wondered why her real mum hadn't been able to keep her? She knew it wasn't the same situation as she had been in with Helen. Was she bullied into giving me away? Did she cry after me once I was gone? Tears slid down Moira's cheeks as she struggled to comprehend what had happened and why it had been kept a secret, especially from her.

Savouring every moment with her son, Moira loved everything about him, his tiny toes, his little fingers that curled around her finger. She was happy being given this chance to be a mum again.

It wasn't something she could talk to Sally about. Sally was really struggling after losing Steven. Moira wondered, did her real mum ever make any connection with her before she had to let her go? It felt weird saying 'mum' about a stranger. She still thought that she was her mother and father's daughter, no matter what she had found out.

Now, she knew the strained relationship between her and her mum was because she wasn't her baby, and the tension between her mum and dad was because she was his baby and not Joy's baby. It was a big sacrifice her mum had made. Tears began to fall, and she cried quietly for a long time with Daniel in her arms.

She had tried to talk to Brian about it, but he was increasingly distant these days. She was trying to work out if it was the long hours he was working or the sleepless nights with Daniel. He was always so short-tempered.

He didn't need to work long hours; they had enough money to take some time off together. He seemed determined to be the breadwinner.

She knew she needed to find out more about where she had come from. Tomorrow, she was going to call the solicitor they had seen in Dumfries to see if he could shed any more light on the story. Heading back to bed, she tossed and turned.

Brian brought her a cup of tea and some toast each morning before he left for work. She looked at him as he came in and smiled. He just got on with things. She was happy and content. Her little family and her little ground-floor flat were just perfect.

Calling the solicitor's office later that morning, once Daniel had gone for a nap. She was sad to hear that Sandy Grey had passed away. A secretary said she would try to locate the file.

She called Sally next to see what she was up to.

"Hey Sally, would you like to come over for the weekend again?" Moira asked.

Sally happily agreed. Sally had been at the University of Caledonia in Glasgow for the past eight months. Moira hadn't seen much of her. Sally kept saying she was busy and that she was mixing with her uni friends.

"Brilliant, it feels like ages since we last saw you, Daniel is so big now," Moira paused, deciding not to say too much else about Daniel.

Sally had come to the hospital to see him, but had rushed out in tears. Brian had gone to see if she was okay.

Daniel was almost six months old. He was still a noisy baby, but much more settled and in a good routine. Motherhood sat well with Moira. She loved her little boy dearly.

It was all arranged. Sally was coming over to stay the weekend. Moira gave a little skip of delight. Brian and Sally got on like a house on fire, so it wouldn't be a problem to let him know later.

Telling Brian over tea that night, she could see that he wasn't as happy about Sally coming as she thought he would be. But he said it was fine and that he was looking forward to seeing her again.

Moira went to meet Sally off the underground at Ibrox station with Daniel. Taking the pram from Moira straight away, Sally was delighted to see Daniel.

"He is so handsome, just like his daddy," Sally said cooing into the pram.

They chatted all the way home about her course and how she was feeling.

Deciding to get fish and chips in for tea as a treat, they had a great chat around the table. Brian went out to get some drinks; it had been a while since Moira had had a drink. She enjoyed the feeling of the whisky and lemonade. It made her feel more relaxed than she had for a long time. Having another one made her feel woozy. She made her excuses and headed off to bed, knowing that she wouldn't manage Daniel with a fuzzy head.

Waking up to Daniel's cries, she looked at the clock; it was 3.30 am. She turned on the lamp and noticed that Brian wasn't in bed. Maybe he had gone to Daniel. Opening the door to the baby's room, Daniel was snuffling away. She picked him up and held him close, making her way to the kitchen to warm his bottle. She could see that the living room lamp was still on. Brian and Sally were wrapped around each other, fast asleep.

Was she seeing things? Her head was a bit groggy. No, it was clear they were wrapped in each other's arms. What on earth were they thinking about? Obviously, they had drunk too much and not made it to bed, but why were they so close, wrapped around each other?

On automatic pilot, she boiled the kettle to warm the bottle. Starting to think that maybe she had imagined it, she made her way back to the living room. Daniel let out a wail, waking the two of them up. Moira watched them unwrap themselves and, in that moment, knew that they hadn't just fallen asleep drunk. Thankfully, they hadn't seen her.

With a wailing, hungry baby, she knew she had to feed him. Snuggled in her arms, drinking the warmed milk, she looked at his trusting, beautiful face. How was she going to deal with this? Putting Daniel back in his cot, she waited till he was fully asleep before leaving the room. The living room lamp was off. Making her way to the bedroom, Brian was fast asleep in their bed.

Knowing in her heart that she would have to confront them about what she had seen made her heart skip a beat. Did she really want to burst her little bubble of family life? On the other hand, did she really want a cheating husband? And as for her so-called best friend! What on earth was going on here?

Moira was first up in the morning. Making herself a strong sweet coffee, she knew she was going to have to say something.

It may be easier to speak to Sally about it first. Making her way down the hall to the living room, her mind was racing with questions she wanted answers to from Sally. Opening the door slowly and quietly, she could see that the room was empty. Sally wasn't on the couch. The blankets and pillow she had left out for her were untouched on the chair opposite.

Scanning round the room, she noticed that Sally's bag was gone as well. Moira felt a wave of hot anger wash over her. Turning round sharply to make her way back to her bedroom, she saw Brian standing in the kitchen doorway.

Looking straight at him, she snarled, "I know what you two have done. How could you? I take it Sally has sneaked off in shame, I hope."

"What are you going on about, Moira?" Brian looked surprised.

"You know exactly what I am talking about, Brian, you and Sally last night, I woke up to feed Daniel, and there you were, wrapped around each other on the couch."

Throwing her a look of disdain, Brian went into the kitchen. She heard the kettle going on and the clinking of cups. Feeling a mixture of anger and fear about the confrontation to come, she made her way to the bedroom and got dressed quickly. She could hear Daniel snuffling in his room; he would be hungry again soon.

"So!" she declared angrily at him, as he sat at the table sipping his coffee.

"Tell me what was going on last night," Moira snapped.

"Nothing was going on last night, Moira. Whatever you think you saw, you didn't."

Brian turned back to his cup of coffee.

"So, you are trying to tell me I imagined seeing you two wrapped around each other on the couch last night," Moira's voice rose.

"We simply fell asleep," Brian's voice was getting louder.

Angry hot tears rolled down Moira's cheeks; she couldn't believe he was in complete denial.

"Why has Sally left then? I would have got the truth from her, she at least had the decency to get out of my house."

"Oh, it's your house, then, Moira, is it?" he snapped back at her.

She wasn't about to let this go. She was seething on the inside, but trying to stay calm on the outside. Scraping back his chair and banging his empty coffee cup on the kitchen counter, Brian made his way to leave the kitchen. Moira stepped to the side to block his way.

"Oh no, you don't just get to walk off," she said.

Grabbing her wrist, Brian twisted her arm hard. She shouted out in pain from the force of it. Moving quickly away from him, she looked at her reddening arm. It hurt. She was shocked that he had hurt her.

The noise of Brian slamming their bedroom door woke Daniel up. His cries knocked her out of thinking about any retaliation or questioning him on what he had just done. By the time she had seen to Daniel, Brian had dressed and slammed out of the front door. It was Sunday. Where was he going? Maybe he was meeting Sally. Moira was furious.

Getting Daniel ready to go out, she grabbed his bag and hers, thinking she would catch up with Brian and Sally.

It was a fruitless journey. Walking around, wondering where they might be. She went to their favourite cafe in Govan, thinking they might meet there. She ate an egg roll and made her way back home. What was she thinking about? She should have stayed in.

As she opened the front door, she could smell burnt bacon; he was back then. Pushing the pram through the door, she felt a pang of fear. What if he was really angry at her for being out all day, what if he had only gone out for his paper and to clear his head?

Leaving Daniel asleep in his pram in the hallway, she ventured into the living room.

"Brian, we need to talk about this," Moira's voice trembled.

Completely ignoring her, Brian turned the television off and headed into the kitchen. She followed him.

"No, we don't, Moira, there is nothing to say, except I am sorry I hurt your arm."

"What are you playing at?" Moira asked, "What's wrong?"

She was struggling to work out why he was so angry.

"Moira, I am sorry, but Sally and I are in love," Brian looked at her sadly.

Tears filled her eyes. What on earth was he talking about? Surely she had not heard him say that.

"Brian, what are you saying? Why? What's been going on? How long?"

The questions all came tumbling out at once. Looking at her husband at the kitchen table, she realised she didn't really know this man. Where had the loving, laughing, kind man gone that she had fallen in love with? Little things started to come to mind about them, how had she not twigged? Why had he married her? Why not just say something? No, instead they just carried on behind her back.

"Why, Why?" she screamed at him.

Tears streaming down her face, she ran out the front door, out into the fresh air. She walked around the block, trying to clear her head. There had been a look in Brian's eyes that told her there was no going back from this.

Her world was crumbling again.

Stopping at the phone box, she dialled the operator's number and asked to make a reverse charge call to Sally's house. She heard Patsy accept the charge.

"Moira, how are you? Is everything ok?"

Blurting out everything to Patsy with tears streaming down her face. She asked if she knew anything was going on.

There was silence on the other end of the phone until Patsy's calm voice said, "Moira, I am so sorry this is happening to you. What can I do to help you?"

Moira slammed the phone down without replying. Slumping down in the phone box, she let out a scream of raw anger. What had she done to deserve this! Becoming aware of the smell of urine around her, she got up quickly. Making her way back to the flat, she was determined to get answers to the raft of questions that she had. As she walked into the hallway, she saw two suitcases.

"Brian, what are you doing?" she asked anxiously.

Making her way to the bedroom, she could see Brian throwing the last of his things into another bag.

"What are you doing?" she asked again.

"I'm leaving you, Moira, Sally, and I want to start a life together. You have plenty of money to start again," he answered coldly.

Stepping past her, he slung his bag over his shoulder and grabbed the two suitcases, heading to the front door. Moving quickly, she got in front of him and shouted in his face.

"There is no way you are just taking off, without telling me what has been going on," Moira was almost hysterical.

"Get out of my way, Moira."

He pushed her hard into the wall, giving himself room to get out of the flat.

Moira was winded and in shock. There was no one here that she could talk to. She wanted her dad. Coming to her senses, she moved on jelly legs. Making her way outside, she watched their little brown car turn at the end of the street. She could see that Sally was in the car too. How had she not seen her when she came in?

She walked slowly back inside with tears in her eyes. Her mind could not fully process what had just happened.

She was glad Daniel had stayed asleep through it all. Closing the flat door, she looked into the pram. It was empty. Running into his room, she saw that Daniel was not there; the drawers were lying open, and most of his stuff was gone.

Dropping to her knees beside his cot, she wailed, "No! My baby. They have taken my baby!"

Sixteen

Facing Facts

Not knowing what think or do. Moira stayed on the bedroom floor; the tears she shed were pure rage. How could they have done this to her? What had she done wrong? Her best friend had been sleeping with her husband. The sound of someone knocking at her front door broke her out of her thoughts.

"Who on earth is that at my door?" she said under her breath.

Opening the door, she saw her neighbour Sheila standing there. Sheila was in her sixties, Moira guessed, she was a dainty lady with dark grey curly hair.

"Moira, are you ok? Sadie said she heard a commotion at yours," Sheila asked.

Bursting into tears, Moira poured out the events of the past twenty-four hours. Sheila took her into the kitchen, sat her down and made a strong cup of hot sugary tea.

"I don't know what to make of it all," said Moira shakily.

Sheila was one of those neighbours who knew everybody and everything. More than once, Moira had been caught at the post office, having to listen to the tales of what was going on in the street.

"What are you going to do about it, Moira? They can't just take your child away like that."

Sheila was adamant that she should call the police.

"I don't know what I can do about it. Is it a crime to take your own child?"

Moira was unsure about what to do next.

Sheila made them both some toast and another cuppa.

"Can I have coffee this time please," Moira asked.

"You need to keep your strength up, young lady. You have had quite a shock."

Sheila reached out to hold Moira's hand.

They chatted for a while, then Sheila said she had to go to pick up her grandson. Thanking her for coming and being there for her, she closed the door behind her with a sigh. Although Sheila was trying to help, Moira knew the whole street would soon know what had happened.

Going into Daniel's room, she pulled the sheet off the bottom of the cot and held it to her nose. Breathing in his scent, she prayed that he would come back to her soon. She never wanted to set eyes on Brian or Sally ever again, but she wanted her son back.

Taking the sheet into the living room with her, she knew she had to call Patsy to let her know what had happened. Sally's mum could not believe what she was hearing.

"Moira, no, please tell me that isn't true, why would she do such a thing?"

Patsy was struggling to take in that her daughter had taken off with Moira's husband and baby.

"I have to tell you, Patsy, that my next call is to the police. I have to find my son. Whatever they want to do, they can go and do it, but not with my son."

The rage was back. Moira was determined to find her baby. She had already lost one child; she wasn't going to let it happen again. It was getting dark now. Closing the curtains and turning on the lamps were habits. Moira looked sadly around the flat. It didn't feel like home anymore; Brian had ripped the heart out of it the minute she realised Daniel was gone.

She was aching to hear Daniel cry, aching to hold him, feed him, anything. Surely they couldn't just take her son away like that.

Making herself a strong coffee, she heard someone at the door again; it was Sheila.

"Moira, would you like me to sleep over with you tonight?. You've had such a shock."

"Yes, that would be so kind of you, thank you, Sheila."

Moira was glad of the company; she was just about to call the police. The moral support would certainly help her.

The policeman listened politely on the other end of the phone. He asked her to sleep on it, in case they came back in the morning. The police asked her to call back the next day if they didn't come back. Feeling it had been a waste of time to call, Moira put the phone down, feeling worse than before she had called them.

"Sheila, do you mind if I go to bed now? I'm exhausted. Please help yourself to anything you need."

"Of course," said Shela, saying she would sleep on the sofa and see her in the morning.

Moira tossed and turned all night, thinking about where her son might be. He could be close by, or they might have taken him as far away as they could. Her heart was sore. She wished her mum and dad were here. She drifted off eventually, feeling totally alone and hurting deeply.

Sheila tapped gently on Moira's bedroom door.

"Good morning, dear. I've made you some breakfast."

Moira watched Sheila make her way in, with breakfast on a tray.

"Thank you so much, you shouldn't have," Moira said, feeling slightly guilty; she hardly knew Sheila, really.

"It's fine, I enjoyed being here, I have never liked being on my own since my Ernie died," Sheila said, making her way out of the room.

The stark realisation began to seep into Moira's tired brain that her life had just literally turned upside down. She could smell the toast; her stomach heaved. Moving around her room, getting her slippers and dressing gown, felt surreal. She could hear the regular street noises, but nothing in her world was regular right now. She wanted to scream and shout, she wanted to smash her dressing table up. Looking at it, seeing only her things on it, where only yesterday there had been evidence of a couple. She struggled to move past it and open the bedroom door.

Pasting on a smile for Sheila, she was so grateful for this lovely neighbour, who was all of a sudden in her house, making her breakfast. She managed to eat the toast and tea with Sheila in the kitchen. It didn't feel quite right that she ate it in her bed.

"I need to go and visit my mother today," Sheila said gently.

"It's ok, I have plenty to do here, Sheila. Thank you so much for last night, it really meant so much to me to have you here."

The tension in her body left the minute Sheila closed the front door behind her. The tears flowed unchecked, hot, angry tears, then slowed to sad tears. Wiping her face with a cold flannel, she made herself another slice of toast and a hot cup of coffee.

Having a shower felt great, the water splashing down her body, the cleansing action felt good to wash those two right out of her life forever. She noticed a bruise on her hip where Brian had slammed her into the wall.

Settling into the living room, she knew she needed to work out a plan to get Daniel back. It was all about getting her son home. It gave her a sharp stab of pain to think about Daniel crying, looking for her. Brian didn't know his routine that well, and as for Sally, how was she going to manage him?

What if they disappeared and she never saw him again? Would he forget her? Of course, he would; he was a baby.

By twelve o'clock, she knew they were not coming back and made the second call to the police. A bored-sounding officer assured her they would send someone round as soon as they could. Moira was surprised to hear the door knock a few minutes later. She wiped her face and opened the door to see Patsy standing there with her arms outstretched.

"I'm so sorry, Moira. How are you doing?"

Even though Patsy was Sally's mum, it still felt comforting to have someone who had known her all of her life beside her.

Listening intently to everything Moira had to say, Patsy was horrified at what Sally and Brian had been doing, and to have taken Daniel was just the worst twist of the knife.

"We need to find out where they have gone and work on getting your son back to you," said Patsy angrily.

"I know, but where do I start?" Moira said with tears in her eyes.

Showing Patsy her bruises from the day before, she admitted she was more than a little bit afraid to go looking for him on her own.

Brian didn't have many family members to try to contact, only the aunt and uncle who had come to the wedding. She didn't have a number for them. Moira called Brian's work and discovered that he had taken three weeks off.

Realising that catching them had triggered a series of actions that they were probably not prepared for was devastating. How was this going to affect Daniel? She was sure that taking him had been on the spur of the moment.

"It's not like he has permission to take him away. I've done nothing to him to want to cause me this much pain. What the hell is wrong with him?" Moira's voice was rising fast.

She wanted to call Sally a few choice names, too, but stopped herself. How could her best friend betray her like this? What was wrong with her? It was only occurring to her that Sally hadn't had any steady boyfriends. How long had this been going on for? Feeling like her head was full of wasps, she went to the drinks cabinet and poured herself a stiff whisky. It felt good as the warm liquid filled her chest. Taking a deep breath, she poured herself another one.

Pouring the second one, she chose to have it with lemonade. Coming in from the bathroom, Patsy looked at her and the glass, raising her eyebrows.

"Would you like a drink?" Moira asked cheekily.

"No, I have the car, Moira. What if we need to go out somewhere?"

Patsy looked at Moira with concern.

Feeling a little bit chastised, she sat down and nursed her drink for a while, trying to work out her next move. It all seemed futile. They had no idea where they could be.

She had to face the hard facts that they were gone.

Seventeen

Repercussions

Moira and Patsy were sitting on the couch, trying to think about where they could have gone. Patsy had called some of her family members to see if they had heard from Sally. No one had heard a thing from Sally. A loud knock at the door made them both jump. Moira opened the door to find two young-looking police officers standing there.

"Good afternoon, Mrs Morrison, you called us earlier about a missing child?"

"Yes, yes, I did, come in."

Moira was flustered; it was all becoming very real. Having the police involved felt a bit scary.

After a few minutes of listening to the turn of events over the past couple of days, the officers assured her they would put out a call to try to locate the missing trio. She felt that they thought it was just a father taking his son to live with him. They suggested she seek legal advice to try to set up an access arrangement, but pointed out that it could be a lengthy process and that, at best, she would only get limited access, and she would need to locate him first.

Feeling utterly defeated, lost and alone in the world, she walked slowly back to the living room after seeing the police officers out. Seeing the look on Moira's face, Patsy suggested that she should come home for a short time.

"No, this is my home now. What if they see sense and want to come back?" Moira said sadly.

It was later that evening that she felt the need for a wee dram. Two whiskies later, she had that warm glow. Patsy had headed back up to Dumfries. She felt she wanted to try to get on with things; there was nothing she could do until they surfaced or got in touch.

She had asked herself every question under the sun as to why this could have happened. The only conclusion she came to was that it had been going on for a long time, she had been blissfully unaware of it, being all caught up with getting married, having a baby and setting up home.

Should she blame herself? She kept thinking back to many moments when things had been tense, they had of course argued, wasn't it normal in any relationship? Maybe she should try to find out who she really is. Since finding out that she had not been Joy's biological child had been a shock, she hadn't really had time to look into it all. Now, on her own, maybe it was time to seek out some answers, give herself a purpose.

She poured another drink as she started to imagine who her other mum might be, what she looked like, and where she lived. Maybe she had siblings; she had always wanted a brother or a sister. It had been lonely growing up on her own.

Starting to feel fuzzy from the whisky, she allowed herself to remember having her first baby in the woods. No one knew she was there. Leaving the baby on the doorstep of the local farmer's house, she had been able to watch her as she grew into a giggly, chubby baby. She began to weep as she remembered hearing that her baby had died in a tragic accident.

Waves of unspent grief flowed into her heart, and she cried herself into a deep sleep on the couch. The next few days followed the same pattern; she wasn't eating or sleeping properly, just drinking whisky till the tears came.

It had been almost two weeks since Brian, Sally and Daniel had left. Moira was not coping; her head was a mess, there was no food in the house, and the whisky had run dry. She had to face going out, not a good prospect, feeling the way she did. Running a hot bath, she put in some lavender bubbles, which made the room smell nice and, she hoped, would make her feel calmer. After a good soak and a wash, she went to the bedroom to find clothes. She hadn't slept in the bedroom since that first night. It felt alien to her.

Getting dressed and doing her hair made her feel physically better. She found some edible food to eat with a coffee; her stomach rolled, but she knew she had to sort herself out. Putting on her coat, she headed out into the street. First things first, she needed some money to see her through the week ahead. She had a lot she wanted to do.

Walking up Copeland Road onto Paisley Road West, she wondered if everyone could see the turmoil she was in. The sensible side of her brain said of course not, nobody even really knows you, Moira. Stepping into the Bank of Scotland, she handed her card to the teller and asked for a hundred pounds.

The teller looked at her with raised eyebrows. Moira looked back at her with a stony glare. She had been in a few times before. The teller asked her to wait there for a moment while she checked something. While she waited, she looked around the bank she loved the high ceilings and the beautiful, large paintings on the walls.

Brought out of her thoughts by the teller's clipped tones asking if she had identification, she rummaged in her bag, bringing out an electricity bill. She felt a brief moment of triumph. She wondered whether the teller was intrigued when she saw how much money she had in the bank. One thing she was happy about was that Brian had no access to this account.

Moira had been advised to open a joint account for daily use and their wages, but to keep the majority of her inheritance in a separate account. The teller placed the money in an envelope and slid it over the counter. Popping the envelope into her bag, she smiled broadly at the teller and bid her a good day. For a brief second, she considered asking for another hundred pounds, just for the hell of it.

After all the tears and anger of the past week, Moira felt a stony coldness growing in her heart. She knew she would continue searching for her son, but she felt nothing but hatred toward Brian and Sally.

Hearing the low rumble of the underground as she approached Cessnock station, she impulsively decided to head into the city centre. *"Why not?"* she thought? Trying not to trip over her purpled flared trousers, she ran down the steps of the station into the dank-smelling depths of the underground.

Getting off at Buchanan Street, she made her way up to Sauchie-hall Street and began to meander around the shops. Buying herself some perfume and a dress, she headed to the toilets in Frasers to change into the dress.

Feeling a bit of devilment, Moira decided to go into a bar on her own. She needed a drink. Sitting there nursing a whisky and lemonade, she felt a bit strange. She had never really been to a bar, never mind on her own. Looking around, she could see that she was in the minority.

Two older couples had ordered food. They made Moira feel sad. There were four men together, laughing at something that made her feel even more miserable.

She noticed a young guy with long hair sitting alone to her left. He looked sad too.

Deciding to have one more drink before she made her way home, she made her way to the bar.

"A whisky and lemonade, please," said Moira politely.

"Hey, let me get that for you," the long-haired guy had appeared beside her. He smiled and asked if it was ok if he bought her a drink.

Flattered, she smiled back, saying, "Yes, that's ok, thanks."

They made their way back to her table.

"I'm Tony. What's your name?"

"Moira," she answered shyly.

Chatting for a while, Tony told her he had just broken up with his partner. He lived in Govan on his own.

After a few more drinks, they decided to go to a club for a dance. Moira was feeling quite giddy with the amount of alcohol she had drunk.

They danced a few times. She was enjoying the attention. Tony seemed nice. He worked at Babcock's in Govan and lived pretty close to where she lived. He had a cute moustache, the same colour as his mousy brown long hair.

"Allow me to take you home, Moira. It's getting late."

Moira quite happily let him put his arm around her as they made their way to Buchanan Street underground. They stumbled out of Ibrox station just after 11 pm.

"Where am I taking you, Moira?" Tony asked.

"Copeland Road, please," she said, smiling up at him.

Feeling quite drunk by the time they reached her place, she struggled to get her key in the door.

"I'll help you."

Tony opened the door and helped her into the living room. It was dark; she hadn't left a light on.

As soon as she sat on the couch, he was on her, kissing her fiercely.

"Wait, wait a minute!" she protested.

Moira tried to move away from him, but he was having none of it. He locked his arm around her waist and continued to kiss her, covering her mouth with his.

He began to touch her breasts. This was not what she wanted at all. He was too strong for her, even though she was protesting; he carried on, moving his hands up her legs, pulling her dress up around her waist. Closing her eyes, she gave up trying to stop him.

She felt him pull her underwear off, he entered her and began to pound at her with force.

It didn't take long for it to be over. Breathing a sigh of relief, she opened her eyes to see him already up on his feet. In the dim light, she could see him pulling his trousers back on. Tears pricked her eyes. What had just happened? He didn't even look back at her; he let himself out of the front door. Moira jumped up, locked the door, and put the chain on. She felt sick.

Throwing her clothes in the wash basket, she ran a bath. Oh, my God, what's going on with me? she said to herself. The bath helped her feel slightly better. She knew she shouldn't have gone out into the city by herself, and she definitely knew that she should not have brought him back to her flat. Even though Moira knew she had been raped, she felt like it was her own fault.

She felt sore and disgusted with herself. A wave of nausea came over her. Running to the bathroom, she threw up into the toilet bowl. Hugging the bowl, she cried for a while. She was physically and mentally exhausted.

Getting up, she poured herself a glass of water from the kitchen tap. Drinking half of it, she headed off to her bed with the glass. She slept right through till ten o'clock the next morning.

Moira spent the day tidying up the flat and buying some groceries to make herself a nice meal. By evening, she was starting to feel more positive about moving forward. She poured herself a large whisky and lemonade to reward herself for a good day's work.

She knew that she couldn't stay here. What if Tony remembered where she lived? Bile rose in her throat thinking about what he had done the night before to her. Picking up the phone and pouring herself a drink, she called Patsy.

Telling her everything, she wailed down the phone, "I need to come home, I'm not safe here."

Patsy reassured her that everything would be ok. She would make her way up to Glasgow in the morning and bring her back to the village.

"Thank you, Patsy," Moira said.

Putting down the phone, she let out a huge sigh of relief.

Just as she poured her second drink, she heard her doorbell ring. *"Oh, that will be Sheila,"* she thought to herself, it will be nice to catch up. She felt happy that Sheila was a good neighbour for checking up on her. She opened the door with a smile.

Seeing Tony standing there made her heart leap into her throat. She tried to slam the door in his face, but he was too quick for her. Barging his way in and locking the door behind him, he pushed Moira into the wall.

"What are you doing here? Get out of my house, you bastard."

Moira's heart was hammering in her chest. She felt raw fear as she looked into his eyes; she knew he wasn't about to leave quietly. She tried to wriggle free. Tony punched her soundly in the face. Shocked, she slid down the wall to the floor.

He hissed in her ear, "Shut up, or there will be worse to come."

Frightened, she said, "What is it you want?"

She offered him money; she still had over £70 in her bag. He didn't speak; he just kept looking at her. He had pulled her back up to her feet. He was tall and muscular, no match for Moira's slight frame at 5'2". Moira could feel blood running from her nose; she moved her hand to wipe it away. Grabbing her arm, he slammed it into the wall above her head and started to kiss her roughly.

"No… No… Oh God, no…!"

Moira felt the terror rising in her body.

Dragging her by the hair into the bedroom, Tony threw her onto the bed and started to undress himself. Pleading with him, she begged him to leave her alone. Moving over to the bed, he grabbed at her clothes, wrestling them off, throwing them across the room, moving on to her he started to squeeze her breasts. Putting his hand between her legs, he began to finger her roughly. Moira cried out in pain as he continued to thrust his fingers into her.

No, Please stop. Moira pleaded.

Tony hit her hard across the face again.

"Be quiet," he shouted as he got on top of her.

Thrusting himself into her, she lay as limply as she could, praying it would be over soon. Turning her over and pulling her up towards him he shoved her face into the bed, he held her arms behind her back as he continued to pound into her. Her mind went blank. Pain and fear were coursing through her body.

With one final judder, she thought it was over, but he threw her onto her back again and spat in her face.

"You slut. You asked for this."

Moira was terrified. Thinking he was going to kill her she let out a scream? It made him furious. She thought briefly of Daniel.

He pulled her off the bed and into the kitchen. He raped her again. Moira was in agony. Tony dragged her naked body into the hallway, pushing her up against the wall.

He took her hair in his hand while his other hand was squeezing her neck.

"Don't make another sound," he said in her ear.

She knew she was going to die right here in the hallway. The crazed look on Tony's face told her she was not going to survive.

She felt sad that her life was ending this way. But, pleased to not be on her own anymore.

Everything went black.

Eighteen

I'm Alive

Coming round, Moira couldn't believe she was still alive. A shard of abject terror went through her heart as she wondered if he was still in the flat. As she had passed out, his rage-filled face had been the last thing she had seen. It was a face she knew would never leave her.

She tried to stand up, but searing pain was everywhere. Her ribs, her back, everywhere, inside and out, pain engulfed her every move. What had he done to her while she was unconscious? She didn't want to think about that.

She crawled into the living room with no idea of what time it was. Dialling 999, she managed to tell someone she had been attacked and needed an ambulance. She could see that she was bleeding onto the carpet. Where was it coming from?

Thinking that she should try to get to her bedroom to put on her housecoat at least, she passed out where she was beside the couch. Hearing the siren of the ambulance outside was the last thing Moira heard till she woke up in the Southern General hospital a week later with a nurse at the side of her bed.

"What's going on? Where am I?" Moira called out.

Trying to sit up, it all came flooding back to her. Tony's ugly, angry face appeared in front of her.

Reaching out for the nurse, she asked her, "What has he done to me?"

The nurse held her hand for a moment and explained that she had extensive injuries, but that she would get the doctor to come and speak to her.

Tears began to roll down Moira's face; she almost wished she weren't alive. It was all her fault anyway, she shouldn't have taken him to her flat.

A few minutes later, the young nurse arrived back with the doctor. He looked very serious with his dark horn-rimmed glasses and slicked-back grey hair. Pulling up a chair, he sat down and began to tell her about her injuries. She had three broken ribs, a fractured jaw, and multiple areas of deep bruising, including some serious internal injuries. Moira instantly felt sick. She started heaving, but the only thing that was happening was more pain.

The doctor prescribed her something she had never heard of to calm her down and help her sleep. She needed time and sleep to continue the healing process. The nurse pushed a syringe into the cannula in her hand. She drifted off into pain-free unconsciousness.

Nineteen

Heading Home

Moira smiled as Patsy walked into the ward. After days of drifting in and out of sedative-induced sleep, she felt ready to see Patsy. The ward staff were lovely, but they didn't know her. Patsy tried and failed to hide the horror on her face as she took in all the bruising on Moira's face and neck.

"Oh my Gosh, Moira, you poor soul, I'm so sorry this has happened to you. I feel awful. I shouldn't have left you."

"It's not your fault some lunatic did this to me, I should never have gone out on my own anyway," Moira reassured her.

"Are the police any closer to catching him?" Patsy asked hopefully.

"I really don't know, I've not seen them since I gave my statement. Let's hope so. We don't want him to do this to anyone else."

Moira was horrified at the thought of him doing this to someone else.

"When do you think they will let you out of here?" Patsy asked.

"I think they just want to be sure my ribs are healing and my jaw, then hopefully I can go home," Moira replied.

"You are not going back to that flat, Moira; you must come home to us for a while. We would love to have you at ours." Patsy said.

"We have given notice to the tenants in your house. You will need to stay with us for a week,"

Patsy looked at Moira. She felt a deep sadness and a deep sense of guilt that her daughter had triggered the events that had led to the attack.

"Has there been any sign of Brian and Sally? Do they know what happened to me?"

Moira wanted to know.

Hesitating for a moment, Patsy wondered if now was the right time to tell Moira that they had left the country and they were in Southern Ireland somewhere.

She decided not to say anything for now, but shrugged her shoulders and said blithely, "They will crawl out of the woodwork soon enough. No, I've not heard anything from them."

After chatting for a while, they discussed plans for her to return to the village.

"Do people know what has happened?"

Moira was anxious about people knowing too much.

"Yes, Moira. People know your marriage is over and that you have been attacked," Patsy said sadly, knowing the village gossips would be having a field day at Moira's expense.

Moira felt a stab of fear at the thought of leaving the hospital. She felt strangely safer here, even though the ward noises were keeping her from a good night's sleep, and as for the smells, enough said! The food wasn't too bad. She was able to eat a bit better now that the swelling in her face had subsided.

Patsy had left with a cheery wave as soon as the matron rang the visiting bell. She was staying with a friend of hers in Glasgow until tomorrow. Thinking about going home did not appeal to Moira; there wasn't any comfort there anymore. Her parents were long gone, her best friend was gone. The thought of having to explain all of her reasons for being back didn't really bear thinking about. But maybe she needed some familiarity to help her get her life back on track.

She called the nurse over as she walked by. The nurse was called Carol. She was young, with flaming red, curly hair that she struggled to keep under her paper hat. She smiled at Moira as she made her way over.

"Are you ok, Moira? How can I help you?"

Moira had made a connection with her. Carol had been there from the day she was admitted.

"I really want to go home. Could you ask the doctors in the morning if I can go home?" she pleaded.

"Are you sure you should even be going back to that flat?"

Carol pointed out that it would not be in her best interests to ever go back there.

"The team would need to make sure you had the proper support in place before we could release you,"

Carol assured Moira she would ask the doctor in the morning.

Moira knew she wanted to go home; her thoughts were caving in on her. The doctors were going to get seriously fed up with her asking till they let her out. She was getting around much better, and her internal injuries were healing well. Bruising was now a browny-green colour.

Going back to the flat was not an option. Moira never wanted to see Copeland Road ever again. The police had been in to tell her that there was no trace of her attacker anywhere. All their leads had fallen flat; no Tony was working at Babcock who fitted the description she had given.

Her only option was to go back to Glendoon. She knew it would be tough going back with her tail between her legs, so to speak. But what other plan did she have? The thought of starting again somewhere new terrified her.

She hated even thinking about him; it brought back feelings of utter terror and disgust about what he had put her through. She despised how she felt inside now. Would the feelings of disgust and being dirty ever leave her?

Carol returned to Moira with her evening medication.

"I have left a note with the night nurses to give to your doctor in the morning. Think very carefully before leaving the hospital, before you are ready. I'm not on duty tomorrow, so please at least stay until I'm back on shift," and shouted, "Night, Moira," with a cheery wave as she left the ward.

Smiling Moira made a noncommittal noise and took her medication. Drifting off to sleep, her last thought was, where would she go? Doctor Fraser was early on his rounds the next morning.

"Hello there, Moira, how are we feeling this morning?"

He had a quick survey of her physically.

"I want to go home," she said, looking at him with her best pleading face.

"Dr., I really do feel like I could go home."

He sat on the end of the bed, giving her a look that Moira interpreted as if she was nowhere near ready to go home.

"Moira, you have had a real shock to your system. Yes, the physical side is healing nicely. But the mental scars will be long-lasting, and it will be a long time before you get over what has happened to you. We would need to arrange a counsellor and ensure you were moving to a safe place. Not only have you endured this attack, but you have also got to deal with the fact that you have lost your family too."

Dr Fraser was worried about her.

Trying to hold back tears, Moira asked him how long it would be, as she wanted to get back to reality and move on.

"I'm stronger than you think," she said weakly.

Dr Fraser sighed and said, "Okay, Moira, let's get some things in place, a safe place to stay and some counselling sessions in place at least. I will arrange for a psychiatrist to come and speak to you to determine where you are mentally."

"How does that sound?" he continued, as he began to move to the next bed.

Breathing a sigh of relief, Moira started to cry. She was elated that getting home was in reach, but frightened about how she would cope.

Patsy had brought her some clothes last week, and getting dressed and feeling comfortable had taken a few days. Choosing a nice blue top and a pale blue skirt, she felt almost normal when she came back from the bathroom. Heading to the patients' lounge, she picked up a couple of magazines, found a comfy seat and settled down to read for a bit.

She knew it was around 11 o'clock because of the rattle of the tea trolley making its way down the ward. Sandra was always on time. She popped her cheery face in the door and shouted, "Tea, coffee or juice?"

She always wore her jet-black hair in a bun and wore the brightest red lipstick.

"A coffee for me, please, Sandra. Could I ask you to bring the telephone in when you've finished your round? I have a couple of calls to make, I might be getting out soon."

Moira felt great saying the words 'getting out soon' out loud.

Sandra trundled the payphone into the lounge and plugged it in. Moira dialled the number carefully.

Patsy answered the phone in her usual cheery way, "Hello?"

Moira was quick to say hello back. She had a burning question to ask Patsy. She wanted to know how quickly she could move back into her house in Glendoon.

After a few pleasantries, Moira asked, "How soon can I move into my house?"

Patsy had already pre-empted this, telling Moira that the tenants had been given their notice a couple of weeks ago. She could move in next week.

"Are you getting home soon, Moira?" Patsy asked.

"Yes, I have pestered the doctors, and I think they are happy to let me go home. I have good support in the village, and they have arranged a counsellor for me to see at Cresswell," replied Moira.

"Great news, Moira. Just let me know when you need to be picked up, and we will bring you home."

Patsy asked Moira if she would like her to put the notice in on the flat on Copeland Road for her.

"Yes, please, I know I will never set foot in there again," said Moira, shaking her head at the thought of it.

Moira had asked Patsy to retrieve her clothes and all of Daniel's things. And any paperwork that was lying around or in the drawers. There was nothing else that she wanted from that place.

Patsy asked her if she wanted to go and see if there was anything that she had missed, but Moira was adamant that she wasn't going anywhere near it again. A couple of days later, Patsy brought some clothes and toiletries to the hospital.

"Are you sure you don't want to check the flat, Moira?"

"I'm more than sure, Patsy. Thank you for sorting it all out."

As they said their goodbyes, Patsy reminded Moira to phone the day before she was getting out. The rest of Moira's things were piled high in the car. Patsy would sort it all out for her and make sure she had the groceries in the house she might need to come home to.

Nervous wasn't the right word for how she was feeling as she prepared to leave the hospital. She had grown close to Sandra and Carol; they had both been constant sources of encouragement in her recovery. Patsy would be arriving soon. Moira was feeling apprehensive about returning home. Patsy had reassured her that she had nothing to worry about.

Patsy arrived with a bag full of gifts. Moira wanted to show her appreciation to the staff who had been there day in and day out, and to give something a little special to Sandra and Carol.

Counselling sessions would start at Cresswell Hospital in Dumfries in two weeks, and her old family home had been aired and was ready for her return. Dr Fraser had been pleased with her progress and with how quickly she had managed to sort everything out.

Watching her make her way up the ward, saying her goodbyes, he wondered if she knew how tough her full recovery would be, trauma was a tricky thing to manage, especially knowing that the man who had almost killed her had not been caught and was still on the loose somewhere. He wished her well as she left.

Making her way out to the car, Moira felt a pang of uneasiness. *"Where did that come from,"* she thought. I have nothing to worry about; I'm moving far away from here. But still, a heaviness was pressing down on her. Patsy chattered all the way down the road from Glasgow to Dumfries. It felt weird being in the car heading back to where she came from with the mother of the person her husband was now with.

Still not really able to mentally process that whole situation, she shook her head and laughed at something Patsy was saying, willing the car to go a bit faster so she could be on her own for a bit. The ward had been nice, but she felt stifled and stuck in the same place, with people around her all the time; even going for a bath wasn't private. The door might be shut, but patients were in and out of the bathroom getting washed or going to the toilet, and if she took too long in the bath, one of the nurses would knock and pop their head around the door to politely ask if she was alright.

"Yes," she thought to herself, *"I'm ready for a bit of solitude, space to think, maybe even plan what is next for me."* Doing her best to shake off the heavy feeling, she started asking Patsy some questions about the village and who was still around. Even though it had only been two years since she had been away, it felt like longer.

Patsy pulled up outside her house. Pulling up outside her ex-best friend's house was a tug on the heartstrings. She felt sad, hurt and angry at the same time. She wondered what Patsy really thought of the whole sorry situation. At some point, they would need to have a real heart-to-heart.

Stepping out of the car, she breathed in the fresh air, enjoying the smell of home. Looking around the village, memories came to her, making her smile—the pub where her dad went to get a quiet pint away from her mum. The church spire peeped up from the roofs of the houses across the road. She thought about all the times her mum had forced her to attend services, then made her watch her serve the teas and coffees, instead of letting her go off to play like the other kids. Once or twice her dad had asked to take her home, but no, her mum would have none of it.

"Moira can learn to sit still for five minutes. This is God's day; she doesn't need to be running around the village on a Sunday."

Moira smiled, remembering her mum's acerbic tone. Her dad never asked again.

"Come on then, Moira, let's get a cuppa and some lunch before you go on up to your place."

Patsy guided her into her house. She had made sandwiches before she left for Glasgow. Moira ate quickly and enjoyed a nice hot cup of strong coffee.

The mix of feelings Moira was experiencing as she arrived at her own house later on surprised her. She was relieved to be home but sad that both her parents were gone. She also felt angry that her life had changed so dramatically. Thankfully, not much had changed in the house. It had a fresh lick of paint, new curtains, a new sofa, and new beds, too. A locksmith had been and added a new mortice lock to the front and back doors, and a chain had been put on both too. Window locks had been fitted on all the downstairs windows. She still wondered if she would feel truly safe here.

Would anywhere ever feel safe again? Would she be able to trust again, after being betrayed by the two people closest to her? Questions whirled around in her thoughts as she walked slowly up the path to the familiar front door.

Closing the door after reassuring Patsy that she would be fine, she slid down the front door and wept. The tears just kept coming. She hadn't cried like this even in the hospital. It was like a dam bursting; all the pent-up emotion came flooding out. She wasn't sure how long she had stayed there. Exhausted, Moira got to her feet and took a deep breath. Her life had been blown to smithereens. Now back where she had started her life, starting again felt impossible.

There was no trace of her mum and dad in the house. She would need to get up into the loft and bring down the personal photos and ornaments that would make it feel more like her home again.

Making herself a light sandwich and a well-deserved hot chocolate, she sat in the living room intending to watch a bit of telly. Instead, her mind took her back to many moments in her childhood. The memories were comforting. Finishing off her hot chocolate, she suddenly felt utterly exhausted. She locked the doors, put the chains on and checked all the windows before heading upstairs to her room.

Seeing her room and her parents' old room brought a fresh set of tears. Looking around, it all felt familiar but not as comforting as she had thought it would. Climbing into bed, she decided to keep her bedside lamp on as she lay down to sleep.

Waking up to bright sunshine streaming in the window, it took a moment to remember she was home in the village. It was 10 am. Moira was surprised that she had slept that long. It was probably the best and longest night's sleep she had had since going into hospital.

She hadn't closed any of the downstairs curtains the night before, so the house was full of sunlight. Opening the back door as she put the kettle on, she enjoyed listening to the familiar sounds of the countryside. She had asked to be left alone for a couple of days; she would phone if she wanted any company. It felt a bit selfish, but she hoped that explaining to Patsy how she was feeling would help her understand.

Sitting out on her back step, drinking coffee, she felt more relaxed than she had in months. It was great just sitting quietly in the sunshine on her own. Feeling hungry, she put a couple of rashers of bacon on with some scrambled egg and toast. It all tasted divine. The hospital food she had thought was quite good, but this was really good. Even the smell of the bacon frying made her smile. She enjoyed the moment of feeling almost normal.

After an hour of soaking up the sun, she locked the back door and made her way upstairs. The spare room was almost full of bags from the flat in Glasgow. She looked at them with despair; there were so many. *"One at a time,"* she thought, *"one at a time."* Opening a large blue bag, she saw some of Daniel's clothes, which looked so small. Wiping away tears, she thought about what he would be doing. Was he happy?

After closing that bag and putting it in the hallway, she slowly began going through the other bags, retrieving things she might need and putting more stuff in the hallway. Most of it would need to go into the loft. Her tummy rumbled, stopping her in her tracks. Making a sandwich and a drink, she decided it might be nice to go for a walk. She lived at the end of the village next to the woods, and she felt sure she wouldn't bump into anyone.

Shielding her eyes from the sun, she looked up the hill to the woods, looking forward to a familiar walk.

"What have I done to deserve such a shit life so far?" she said out loud to herself as she locked the front door.

Moving quickly up the hill, she intended to walk off the feelings of misery that washed over her. Reaching the woods, she walked the long way round, taking in all the sights and sounds of the forest. Breathing in deeply, she enjoyed the feeling of freedom and peace in that moment.

Coming to the edge of the woods, she could see the water shimmering in the distance. Moira welcomed Memories of summertime swims in the loch. Lost in a myriad of happier memories, she was suddenly jolted out of them by a beautiful, small, black spaniel trying to gain her attention by jumping up at her.

She heard a familiar voice shouting, "Mickey, Mickey, get down! Oh dear, I'm so sorry, this dog thinks it should get hugs from everybody."

Moira smiled and said, "Hello, Fiona."

Looking up, Fiona was startled to realise that it was Moira who was standing there.

"Moira, how are you? It's so lovely to see you again. Are you here for long?"

"Gosh, Fiona, slow down. Too many questions," Moira smiled, happy to see her friend.

"Yes, I'm back here for a while. Things have been a bit tricky. I'm on my own now," Moira said with a wry smile.

"Oh, Moira, I was so sad to hear about everything that happened to you."

Fiona reached over and gave Moira a side hug.

"I'm on my own, too. Gavin died about eight months ago, less than a year after our little boy was born. Would you like to walk with us for a bit, maybe come in for a cuppa at the farm?"

Looking at Fiona, she happily agreed to walk with her and Mickey and come for a cuppa.

"Where is your little one, What's his name?"

Moira hoped to meet Fiona's son.

"He is at nursery today, and we called him Tommy,"

Fiona's face beamed happiness.

"Can I ask what happened to Gavin?" Moira asked.

"Of course you can, he died of a sudden heart attack. He was in Dumfries having a pint with his friends. There was nothing anyone could do; at least he died happy," Fiona said with a smile tinged with sadness.

Making their way back down the hill to the farmhouse, Moira looked around and sighed. It was comforting to be back home, but the sense of profound loss and pain threatened to overwhelm her in that moment.

Being immediately transported back to that terrifying moment when she left Helen on the farmhouse step, as she spotted the bucket she had kicked to bring someone to the door.

"Come on in, Moira," said Fiona as she opened the door.

The warmth from the kitchen range was just what she needed. Spotting a photo of Helen on the mantlepiece brought an unexpected tear to her eyes. It had been easy sometimes to put Helen to the back of her mind, in the midst of everything else.

Picking up the photo, Moira asked if Fiona had anymore.

"Yes, we have a few. Would you like one?"

Hesitating for a moment, wondering if that would be a good idea, eventually she whispered out a quiet "Yes, please."

It felt good chatting to Fiona over a nice hot coffee, knowing the loss Fiona had suffered helped Moira to open up to her. They spent the whole afternoon catching up on village stories and sharing their own stories of recent events.

Making her way back along the lane to the house, Moira felt fairly settled. It was good to have spent time with Fiona. They had enjoyed a hearty bowl of homemade broth with crusty bread before she had left, so she didn't need to think about dinner. Letting herself into the house, she wanted to call out, 'I'm home' but knew no one was there. A wave of deep sadness washed over her as she locked the door behind her.

Settling down to watch television, she poured herself a whisky and lemonade. Only a small one, it had been ages since she had had a drink. It felt good making its warm way down her neck into her stomach. She made the second one a bit stronger.

TWENTY

MEETING MARIEANN

As she sat quietly in her living room, her mind drifted over to who she was. It had been a shock to learn that one of her parents was not, in fact, her parent. At the time when she had first found out, her brain had nearly exploded thinking about it.

Her name was Moira now, but had it been something else? Had her real mum named her before giving her away? The questions were endless. The main one being Who gave birth to her?

All the questions started to hurt her head. She was tired from overthinking and from being out all day. It was time to go to bed.

Heading upstairs after making sure everything was locked and chains were on, she made a promise to herself to find out who had given birth to her. Someone must know, especially in a small community like this. Flopping down into her bed, she slept soundly again.

The sound of light rain woke her up in the morning. She showered and dressed quickly. Moira ate her breakfast of scrambled eggs and bacon with the back door open; she didn't mind the light rain wetting the linoleum. It was just lovely to be home. It was nice to hear the rain pat, pat, pat on the leaves and branches around the garden.

Her thoughts and questions from the night before were still whirling around unanswered. It was essential to her to at least try to find out who she was and where she had come from. She knew how much it had meant to her to know where Helen was and to be able to see her. Maybe her real mum was local; perhaps she already knew her.

Moira gave her head a shake. Going down the rabbit hole of questions again was not proving helpful. She would need to think about a plan, a way to dig into the past to find out what she could.

Putting her plate and cup in the sink, she made her way to the spare room, where there was still a load of boxes to go through. She knew one of them had lots of paperwork in it. Some from when she had cleared out drawers after her dad had died. She had never really looked through any of it properly. Daniel, coming along, had taken over her life; she had thrown herself completely into motherhood, so happy to have that second chance at having a child.

Finding a box of photographs in the first bag, Moira was transported back to happier times with her dad. It became apparent to her as she sifted through the photos that there were very few of her with her mum. Sitting cross-legged on the floor, looking at one of the few pictures of her with her mum, she realised it was probably because she spent more time with her dad growing up. Now she knew why.

It became pretty apparent that Joy had not been a happy woman. Moira could not find a single picture except their wedding photo, where her mum was actually smiling.

Marieann was bustling around the room as usual when Moira came in. Moira wasn't sure if it was a tactic her counsellor was using to make her feel more at ease. This was Moira's third counselling session, arranged by the consultant. Marieann was an older, slightly plump lady who smelled strongly of stale perfume.

Moira watched as Marieann made her way eventually to sit opposite her, marvelling at how black her hair was in an old-fashioned beehive style. The first two sessions had been a getting to know each other effort. Marieann had let her know that this session would be different; they would start to look at the trauma she had endured.

The sessions were in a small room at Cresswell Hospital in Dumfries. The room was very impersonal: a brown round table with two green chairs, a wastepaper bin, and a box of hankies. Thankfully, Marieann always had fresh flowers on the table, which brightened up the dull room. The small window had frosted glass, which provided a sense of privacy, but Moira always wondered what it would look out on if it weren't frosted.

Moira had twenty sessions booked with Marieann, with more being available if she felt she needed them. Today, Moira felt a bit worried, knowing it was time to start talking about what had happened and to try to unpick the damage, if that was possible.

The session flew by; it hadn't been as hard as she thought to start talking about everything. She did feel a bit washed out, though. Heading down into town after her sessions was the real highlight of coming into town. Making her way to the Sands, to sit by the River Nith, was comforting while she ate her lunch. There was one bus out of the village and one bus back in two hours.

Watching the seagulls hover and swoop, waiting for the slightest hint of a crumb, made her smile. There was no way they were getting any of her lunch.

In the past couple of months, she had asked a couple of her mum's friends if they knew anything about her adoption. They had all been shocked to hear that Moira was adopted. None of them seemed to know a thing about it. One of them had apparently remembered Joy being pregnant and Moira's triumphant arrival home. They had waited a long time for a child.

Finding out that the solicitor who had dealt with the will and possibly knew more about the adoption had passed away was a blow. She had no way of accessing any files he might have had.

As the River Nith rushed on to wherever it was going, Moira started daydreaming about who she might be. Maybe she was even royalty, maybe her real mum was more like Patsy or Marieann, which would be nice. She often wondered if her real mum thought about her at all. Was there someone out there desperately thinking about how she could find her? Maybe she had brothers and sisters. Growing up as an only child, she would love to find out she had siblings.

Jolted out of her musings by a seagull swooping down and stealing the last bit of her sandwich, she laughed at its audacity. Her next port of call was the high street; she was aiming to treat herself to a new outfit and some shoes. Thankfully, money was not an issue. She still had thousands in the bank from her sudden inheritance.

TWENTY-ONE

MEETING BELLE

Learning to drive and buying herself a little car were next on her list of things to accomplish. Marieann had set her some tasks; one of them was to set short- and long-term goals. She wanted that bit of independence; relying on other people's kindness was fine, but she knew she wanted to be able to get to places herself or even take off in the car for the day to somewhere new. Knowing that if and when she found out where her family was, she wanted to be able to simply get up and go.

Tidying up her lunch stuff and moving off the bench, she noticed a little yellow car in the car park with a for sale sign on it. Yellow was one of her favourite colours. The car looked like a little bubble. Noting down the telephone number on the sign, she made her way up to the shops for a little bit of well-needed retail therapy.

Once she was safely in the house with the lights on and the doors locked, she retrieved the number from her pocket to call about the little yellow car she had her heart set on. Disappointed with no answer, she put the receiver down after letting it ring and ring for ages. She would try again in the morning. Moira settled down to watch TV with a drink after her tea.

Calling the car's number again in the morning proved more fruitful. The car had been owned by a young woman named Susan, who had gone off to university in Glasgow and didn't want to attempt city driving. Her brother Stuart was selling it on her behalf.

Moira phoned Patsy to ask if she could take her into Dumfries to look over the car.

Pulling up at the sands, they saw a tall, blonde young man waiting beside the car.

"That must be Stuart. Isn't he tall?" said Patsy.

The car was inspected inside and out; it was in excellent condition. His sister had looked after it well. It was a Volkswagen Beetle. Stuart had enjoyed sharing all the significant facts about it, even going so far as to tell them that a film had been made about a Volkswagen Beetle called the Love Bug. His oversell approach wasn't needed. Moira had fallen for the car straight away.

Stuart very kindly offered to drive it to the village for them later that afternoon, with his friend following him to bring him home again. Handing over the check for the car and saying their goodbyes, they made their way home. Moira now had to learn to drive. It would be a good distraction to have something to aim for.

Life was moving on for her bit by bit. Six months had passed since she had moved back home. She was getting better at driving her little Beetle; she had named her Belle. Her counselling sessions were going well. But, frustratingly, she was no further forward in trying to find out where she had come from. Someone suggested going to Edinburgh, where they kept all the birth records; she could uncover something there. She had very little to go on; she only really had her date of birth, 16th of May 1951.

Passing her driving test had been the highlight of her week. Patsy had been taking her out every day for an hour for the past six months to help her get the hang of the roads around Dumfries. She could now drive anywhere, including to the records office in Edinburgh, if she wanted to.

The thought of going through the painful process of discovering who she was felt daunting, but she knew she had to do it. There was a need to know burning through her soul.

Today, she was heading into Dumfries to meet the secretary from the solicitors her mum and dad had used as executors, hoping against hope that this woman might know what had happened to all the files when Mr Grey had passed away. This meeting could give her the breakthrough that she wanted, or she could walk away still knowing nothing of the mystery that was Moira.

Dressing carefully and putting her long, dark hair up for a change, she headed out to the car to drive into Dumfries. The drive was lovely. The sense of freedom felt amazing.

They had decided to meet at the clock tower in the centre of Dumfries. Mrs Kirkpatrick was an older woman with grey curly hair. She was tall and slim with an interesting amount of chin hair. Moira struggled not to gape at the long white hairs poking out of her chin and from a large, dark mole on her cheek.

After exchanging a few pleasantries, they decided to sit outside beside the fountain to talk. Mrs Kirkpatrick was quietly spoken and keen to help Moira. She began by explaining that, after Mr Grey's death, there had been some confusion about who was responsible for the office building and its contents. He had never married and had no children. She had continued to go in for two weeks after he had died to try to empty the offices and find out who owned the building through checking land registries and any paperwork she could find.

As there was no family anyone knew of, his house and assets were awaiting the courts to find any distant family. As far as Mrs Kirkpatrick was aware, all the clients' files were most likely at the courthouse until things could be worked out and the family found. None of the information was very helpful to Moira.

"Can I ask you a question, Mrs Kirkpatrick? Did he ever take files home and keep them there, or work on them at home?"

"Oh, yes, dear, he often took work home."

They chatted for a while until Mrs Kirkpatrick said she had to go and meet her daughter at the Sands. Moira waved as the secretary made her way down the hill to the main road. A plan was forming in her mind now. First things first, she made her way to the Dumfries courthouse to see if there was any way she could find out more about these missing files. Would she be allowed to look at her own file? Next, she would have to try to find out where Sandy Grey had lived. She should have asked Mrs Kirkpatrick.

There was a lot to do. Arriving at the courthouse, she started to feel a little intimidated by the building itself, never mind the thought of going in to ask about her files. She was armed with strong information from the earlier meeting to impress upon whoever was in charge that she should be given access to her solicitors' files.

Stepping back out into the daylight, she made a little skip of victory. It wasn't a huge victory, but she now knew where all the files were and that she would see her file soon.

Belle was waiting patiently for her at the Sands. Her little car was her pride and joy. She had bought four little yellow and green cushions for the back seat and had furry knitted love hearts hanging from the mirror at the front.

TWENTY-TWO

LETTERS

Always grateful to arrive safely home, she hopped out of the car and up the path to her front door. The postman had been, and she was surprised to see three letters sitting on the welcome mat for her. She hadn't really had much post except hospital letters and bills. These three letters looked a bit auspicious in their dark brown envelopes. Taking them through to the kitchen, she popped the kettle on and leaned against the counter to open them. The first one was from a solicitor in Glasgow; her face paled as she read the contents of the first letter.

Brian knew she was here and wanted a divorce. The letter stated that he was living in Southern Ireland. No address, but just a place name. Well, she certainly did not want to be married to a cheating rat anymore. It annoyed her that he knew where she was, but she didn't know where he was. Her thoughts turned to Daniel; she tried to picture him. He would be walking and talking by now. Her eyes filled with tears at the thought of Daniel calling Sally mum.

There were two more letters to open, and she wasn't sure she wanted to read the other two yet. Making herself a strong cup of coffee, she placed them on the table in front of her as she sat down. After a few sips of her coffee, she reached for the second letter. Opening it slowly, she saw it was from the police in Glasgow. What on earth do they want? She thought as she read that her heart began to race. They were coming down to see her tomorrow with news about what had happened to her. Clutching at her chest, she felt panic rising. Remembering Marieann's routine for moments like these, she took a minute to breathe slowly in through her nose and out through her mouth.

The third letter could wait; there was far too much going on in her mind to navigate the third and largest brown envelope. Opening the back door, she stepped out into the garden to try to process the news from the two letters that she had just read. She breathed in the smells around her and listened to the birds for a moment. Her sessions with Marieann were down to once a month; she had made such good progress. Marieann had left her a number to call in case of an emergency.

"Was this an emergency?" she thought, *"Just maybe it was."*

Looking up at the sky, she asked the top of the trees, "Why now?"

Her heart was racing, anger and fear were coursing through her body, making her start to shake. Making her way back into the house, she sat at the kitchen table to steady her nerves.

It was like an arctic blast to her emotions, even just seeing Brian's name on the divorce letter. Irreconcilable differences! What a flipping cheek.

How could he even be as brazen as to send her this? Anger was rising above the fear she had felt reading the second letter. She would never forgive him for what he had done. The work she was doing with Marieann was helping, but seeing these letters made her realise there was much more to be done.

She had come to terms with the fact that he had taken off with her best friend. But, she would never come to terms with them stealing her son.

The lack of notice of the police visit tomorrow was troubling her. She didn't think she would be able to see the police or go over any information without some support.

Leaving the third letter unopened, she made her way out of the back door, locking it carefully. She made her way down to Patsy's house to show her the letters. Making her way through the main street of the village, she smiled as she passed shops that were familiar to her since she was able to walk. It felt good to be back at home. The thought of the police coming here to see her felt like a bit of a violation of her safe place.

Patsy was sitting out in her garden. Waving as she approached, Moira smiled as she let herself in through the little blue gate. The gate was so low it hardly served any purpose.

"Hi, Moira, what brings you here?"

Patsy was pleased to see her, but she could see straight away that Moira was a coiled spring.

Tears welled up in Moira's eyes as she tried to tell Patsy about the contents of both letters, "These letters have arrived today, Patsy. I don't know what to do."

"Why not give me the letters," said Patsy gently.

Moira sat down as Patsy opened each letter and read through them. Patsy felt a pang of guilt course through her. Sally had been calling her mum regularly once they had settled in Ireland. Patsy knew that Moira hadn't been ready to know about them being in touch. Maybe it was time now.

Patsy had been trying to reason with her daughter about how important it was for Daniel to get to know his actual mum. Sally would only reply that she was his mum now. It was beginning to look like Brian was not all that he seemed. Sally had been sharing with her mum that he had started to become very unpleasant towards her. He had even pushed her into the wall in their kitchen just last week.

Desperately wanting to tell Moira where they were, but feeling anxious for Sally's safety at the same time, it was a horrible position to be in. She had known Moira since she was a baby.

Jolted out of her thoughts, Moira was standing beside her, asking if she was even listening to her.

"Sorry, Moira, I was thinking about something, my mind was miles away. What was that you said?"

Moira repeated her request for Patsy to come over tomorrow to support her while the police came down with whatever the update was on the man who had attacked her.

A thousand questions began to swarm around in Moira's head. She started to feel a bit sick.

"I think I need to go for a walk, Patsy. I will see you tomorrow at mine for this meeting, ok?" she said as she left.

"Of course I will be there, Moira. You take care of yourself. If you need me, ring down, and I will come up."

Patsy watched Moira walk along the street; her heart ached for her. So young to have been through so much.

As Moira reached her own gate, she decided to keep walking. It was still light as she passed the Barnes farmhouse; she hesitated, then stepped in to see if her friend was home. Fiona opened the door and smiled broadly, seeing Moira there.

"Are you ok, Moira? Come away in."

"No, I'm not really okay. Have you got time to chat?"

"Of course I have," said Fiona, "I have just put some bacon on to make a sandwich, come and join me."

Moira marvelled at how strong Fiona was; she continued to manage the farm without her husband and a toddler. Once they had eaten and shared the obligatory small talk. Moira asked her if she could share the letters with her for her opinion. After Moira explained to her how she felt about both letters, she leaned back in her chair and waited for some words of wisdom from her friend.

"Well, if you ask me, I would be calling that number for the police and asking them to meet you in town or at someone else's house. Why take that into your home? That's your haven right now. I think it would be best if they met you somewhere else." Fiona paused before continuing to speak.

"And, as for the divorce letter, if you have no immediate plans to remarry, why make it easy for him over there by agreeing straight away to the divorce? He will be finding things difficult, living in sin with a baby, too. If I were you, I would pop that letter in a drawer for at least three months before even replying to it."

Fiona's straight talking made Moira smile. It made perfect sense, especially with the meeting with the police, not to taint her house with anything to do with the attack. She would call them as soon as she got home to either postpone it or change the venue.

As for the divorce, it was great advice, but she really didn't fancy being attached to him anymore. Fiona had wisely suggested looking into the legal side of the situation, particularly as it concerned Daniel. Maybe agreeing to the divorce would make it harder to contact him, since they were no longer legally married. What rights would they have when they were married regarding the care of Daniel? Thinking about how much her best friend had hurt her made her blood boil. Yes, why should she make it easy for them to move on? And more difficult for her to have Daniel again.

As she marched back to her own house, determined to take matters into her own hands and not just let things happen, she called the number on the letter. She explained to the desk sergeant that it was not convenient for them to meet tomorrow and that they would need to make alternative arrangements for a meeting place, as she did not want any reminder or anyone associated with the attack in her house.

Putting the phone down, Moira did a little air punch of victory. She felt very proud of herself for taking control of that situation. She headed into the kitchen to seek out a cake as a reward.

Now, to take control of the divorce issue. Moira was definitely not going to make it easy for Brian and Sally to marry and live happily ever after with her son; that was for sure.

The solicitor's letter was popped into the top drawer. She wrote a reminder on her calendar to retrieve it in 8 weeks. See how she felt then.

"That will really annoy him," she chuckled to herself.

As she moved to the other side of the kitchen to put the kettle on, she remembered that there was another letter still to be opened. Turning it over in her hands, it was heavy and bigger than the other two letters. There was nothing on the envelope to suggest who it was from, and the postage had been franked, meaning it was possibly official too.

"No, today was just a two-letter day," she sighed to herself.

The third letter would have to wait till tomorrow. She was tired and knew that any more emotionally disturbing news would not be good for her. Calling Marieann in the morning was at the top of her to-do list. Locking all the doors and putting the chains on, she made her way upstairs to get ready for bed. A nice hot chocolate and a film in her pyjamas sounded great to her. Halfway up the stairs, she heard the phone ringing. Who would be ringing her at 8 pm on a Friday? Making her way back down the stairs, she picked up the phone and answered with a cheery hello. Her hello was met with an eerie silence; all Moira could hear was the burring of the line and some background noise.

"Hello, Hello, is anyone there?"

Still no reply. She found it strange but thought no more about it as she got ready for bed.

Settling down in front of the TV with her hot chocolate, she turned her attention to Kojak, who was desperately trying to solve a murder with his lollipop. Waking up with a cramp in her neck, she had fallen asleep in the chair and still didn't know who had committed the crime. The TV was making a horrible fizzing sound with no picture. It must be very late, she thought as she looked up at the clock; it was 2 am. Pushing in the off button on the telly, she headed off to bed.

Twenty-Three

News

It had been almost a week since the letters had arrived. The third letter remained unopened. For some reason, the desire to open it had not been there. Moira was still worried about what the letter might say after the first two.

Her appointment with the police was today at 1 pm in Dumfries. She felt it might be best to wait until this appointment was over and done with, whatever the outcome, before attempting the third letter.

The only drawback from taking Fiona's advice was that she had had to wait so long for this update. There was a fear in the pit of her stomach that leapt up into her throat each time she thought about what the police were going to tell her. The what-ifs were running up and down her spine: what if she had to face him in court, what if he denied it, what if they had the wrong man or what if they were letting her know he was still out there somewhere.

Hearing a horn peep outside, she opened the front door and shouted

"I'm on my way, give me two minutes."

Grabbing her coat and bag, locking the doors and testing them to make sure they were indeed closed and locked tight, she walked down the path in the bright morning sunshine and jumped into Patsy's car.

"How are you feeling?"

Patsy looked at Moira's pale face and patted her shoulder.

"Not great, there is a fear churning around thinking all sorts of things about what they may or may not say to me," Moira replied with a weak smile.

"Well, let's get going then. The quicker we get there, the quicker you will be out of your misery."

Patsy had her own mixed feelings about this meeting, too.

They made their way into Dumfries early to look at the shops and have a light lunch first; it was better than just sitting all morning waiting. One o'clock felt like an eternity coming round. Sitting in the police station waiting to be called through, Moira felt like she was facing a firing squad. She was choking on the fear that kept rising in her chest.

"Patsy, I think I am going to pass out."

Moira had gone as white as a sheet.

"Sit there, I will go and get someone," Patsy said, concerned about what they were about to tell Moira.

She asked at the desk for a glass of cold water and if they could maybe hurry up, as Moira was struggling with the waiting time.

Eventually, they were called through. The corridor was cold and bare. *"What a dreary place to work,"* Moira thought to herself. A young policeman ushered them into a big room with two sofas and a lamp that looked oddly out of place. As they sat down, the door opened, and two familiar faces from Glasgow walked in. Both shook hands with her and Patsy; she could not, for the life of her, remember their names.

"Good morning, Moira. I'm police constable Karen Grainger. We met a few times in the hospital after your attack."

Karen was young with red hair and a face full of freckles. Moira did remember her, but not her name.

"And I'm PC Michael Hemple. Thank you for taking the time to meet with us today."

Karen took hold of Moira's hand and said quietly, "Moira, we have news about the man who hurt you. This might be difficult to hear."

In that moment, Moira could see his face, the evil look, the long hair, and the smell of his breath flooded her nostrils again. She took a sharp intake of breath.

"Are you ok?" Karen asked.

"Yes, yes, I'm ok, the mention of him has brought back vivid memories, but please carry on," Moira said.

Clearing his throat, Michael began to speak.

"The man who attacked you was called Tony Fairview. He lived in Govan, and at the time, he had just lost his parents and his brother in a car accident. What I have just told you in no way excuses what he did to you. But, we do need to let you know that he took his own life three weeks ago."

"How do you know that it was him?" Moira asked.

"He left a note detailing the attack and how he met you initially. There are facts in there that only he and you would know," PC Hemple paused to let Moira grasp what he had said.

Bursting into tears, Moira could barely take in what she was hearing. It was so unfair. Why had he attacked her like that? Now he was dead, and no justice would happen. Being dead wasn't any justice; it was a peace that he now had that she knew she would never have.

Giving Moira the time she needed to process the news, Karen continued the conversation, "Moira, we have a letter here from Tony. It has been written to you by him as part of his suicide note. We have read it and we felt it might help you. There is, of course, no pressure to read it at all. But we will leave it, maybe with Patsy for now, since we have a copy on file in Glasgow. Is there anything that you would like to ask us?"

There was an avalanche of questions; of course, she had questions. But, Moira's head was in a jumble of incoherent thoughts; she couldn't have put a sensible sentence together if she tried. Shaking her head was all she could manage as the tears silently rolled down her cheeks.

"Are we finished?" Moira asked through her tears.

"Yes, there isn't much more to say, except that the case will now be closed."

Handing the letter from Tony to Patsy, P.C Hemple got up and opened the door for them to leave.

"We know this is no consolation to you, Moira, and we are deeply sorry that we were unable to track him down first. We hope the letter, if you read it, might help," Karen said with compassion.

Leaving the police station and coming home went by in a blur. Moira's thoughts were in a mess. A thousand questions were now flying around inside her mind. Staring out of the car window all the way home, she could make no sense of what she had just been told. It was a random attack from an otherwise fairly regular fella, who had lost his mind in the grief of losing his parents and brother.

Moira had just been in the wrong place at the wrong time. Even more so, the feelings of anger towards Brian and Sally were building up again, because if they hadn't taken off the way they did, she would never have gone out that night.

Now she had two letters that she didn't particularly want to read. Knocking her out of her thoughts, Patsy's voice broke into her thoughts, apologising for not being able to come in and sit with her as she had another appointment. Moira asked Patsy to keep Tony's letter and read it first.

Stepping out of the car into the delicate drizzle of rain that had started falling. She wanted to scream and scream as loud as she could to let the world know how angry and upset she was. She wanted everyone to know how hurt she was, how scared of the future she was. Would she ever be able to trust someone again?

Allowing the hot tears to mingle with the cool, fine drizzle of rain, she walked slowly up the path and let herself in. She threw her bag at the couch with a force strong enough to knock some bits out of the bag onto the floor.

It was only four o'clock in the afternoon, but she knew she wanted a drink. Pouring a large whisky for herself, she downed it in one mouthful, marvelling at how hot a cold drink could feel on the way down her throat. Taking a deep breath, she poured another large one, filling the glass up with lemonade.

By eight o'clock, she was feeling pretty lightheaded and stumbling out of the living room where she had been sitting in a daze, trying to make sense of everything. She knew she needed to eat something. Not feeling up to cooking, she made herself a sandwich with some of the post office's finest homemade raspberry jam. She didn't like strawberry jam or strawberry-flavoured anything. She smiled to herself that the jam was raspberry.

Twenty-Four

The Third Letter

With no recollection of how and when she had gotten to her bed, she woke up with a pounding headache. Rubbing the side of her head, she knew she had one too many the night before. In a panic, she shot out of bed, thinking, Did she lock the doors before she went to bed? The fear made her chest contract. She rushed downstairs to find both doors locked, with their chains on. Her head protested at the sudden, fast movements.

Remembering the news from yesterday, knowing her attacker was never going to hurt her again, but she knew that maybe someone else could. She didn't feel safe, even in her tiny village.

The kitchen was beckoning, paracetamol and coffee were first. Breakfast didn't seem very appealing yet. Taking the coffee into the living room, she opened the curtains to see that the day was going to be a wet one; steady rain was tapping the windows, and all she could see were heavy, black clouds. *"Great, I can't even walk this hangover off,"* she thought. Settling into the couch, she lifted the coffee to her lips to see off the foul-tasting paracetamol when her eye spied a letter on the chair opposite. Puzzled, she wondered what it was doing there.

Retrieving the letter, she could see it was the third letter from the week before that she had been too afraid to open after the other two. It was open; she must have been going to read it, or maybe she did read it. She didn't even remember getting the letter last night.

Today may be the day to see what mystery this letter holds. Should she eat first?

"Oh, Moira, just get on with it," she said out loud, feeling a stab of apprehension, as she pulled the letter out of the brown envelope.

It had been folded in half. It was three pages long, typed on thick paper. There was a company name at the top of the letter. It was a solicitor from Glasgow. James Cassidy & Sons.

"Oh God, what now!" she exclaimed.

Miss Moira Kirkwell,

We are writing to inform you that you have been invited to a meeting with Mrs A Marshall on the 16th of October at 2 pm in our offices at 27 Sauchiehall Street, Glasgow. We are, at this time, unable to provide any further information, but would like to emphasise that it would be in your best interests to attend this meeting.

Yours sincerely, Robert Cassidy

What on earth was this all about? The other pages included a map showing where to find the offices, the nearest subway station, and some legal terminology about the contents of the letter.

Why on earth would she want to go and meet Mrs A Marshall? Leaving the letter on the couch, she made her way to the kitchen to get something to eat. It would have been just as easy to have a hair of the dog that bit her, but sense said eat and rest. Her mind was completely overloaded.

The rain was running down the kitchen window, little trickles racing each other to the windowsill outside. Watching them chase each other down the window eased her tired mind a bit. Once again, so much had happened to her in such a short space of time. Moving away from the window, she knew she had to call Marieann; her head was full of wasps, all vying for space to buzz around her thoughts.

Thankfully, Marieann answered the phone after a couple of rings. She listened patiently as Moira told her everything that had happened.

"Why don't you come in this afternoon, Moira? I have no appointments after three o'clock?"

"Yes, I think I will, I really need to talk this through properly."

Putting the phone down, Moira breathed a sigh of relief.

Driving into Dumfries was treacherous; the rain was lashing down now. Belle was struggling to keep the windscreen clear. She loved her little yellow Beetle. Just going out in the dark, rainy afternoon and seeing her sitting waiting for her in her bright yellow coat brought a smile to Moira's face. She should buy herself a yellow jacket to match the paint on her car she thought.

By the time she raced through the hospital car park, her hair was soaked, and her shoes were wet too. There was nothing like being soaked to dampen the spirit.

Marieann was waiting for her with a lovely hot cup of coffee and some biscuits.

"You look pale, Moira. How are you doing?" Marieann smiled at her wet patient.

Admitting to being very intoxicated the night before, Moira launched into the letters saga; it was a full twenty-five minutes later that she stopped talking. Marieanne gave her a little telling-off, telling her she should have called her when she received the divorce papers. Explaining that she had thought about it, but had spoken to her friend Fiona instead. Moira filled Marieann in on Fiona's advice.

Approving of Fiona's sound advice, Marieann reminded Moira of some techniques she should use daily to combat the overwhelm she was experiencing.

"The choice is yours, Moira, keep them waiting or get your closure for yourself."

"What about Daniel? I don't want to sign my rights away," Moira answered.

"I think taking the whole circumstances into consideration, you have a good chance of fighting for your little boy, get a good solicitor and fight for custody as part of the divorce settlement."

Marieann reminded Moira that times were changing fast, it was the seventies, it wasn't always the man getting his way with everything.

Moira was already starting to feel the brain fog thin out a bit. She was so grateful for these sessions.

"I have the letter from Tony to read as well. What do you think about him writing the letter?"

Looking intently at Moira across the table, she marvelled at this strong, young woman. She had endured so much in such a short time.

"I think that it is something you should consider very carefully, making sure you are in the right place with the right people, before you read it. You can always read it here," Marieann said, smiling gently at Moira.

"What about this mystery letter from the solicitors in Glasgow? What could that possibly be? Have you called them to ask? Maybe you should phone and see if they can give you a little bit more insight into why they want you to come. Possibly take a friend with you if that's allowed," Marieann advised.

Knowing how much Moira had going on was concerning Marieann.

Making the appointment for a week's time to read the letter Tony had written gave her a sense of impending closure on that awful time in her life. Moira thought that it might be helpful to get it over and done with quickly. She had asked Patsy to read it first, anyway, just in case it wasn't going to be helpful.

Making her way out of Cresswell, she was glad to see the rain had stopped. Getting into her car, she decided to go into town to get herself a yellow raincoat to match Belle.

Twenty-Five

Patsy

Rain was one of Patsy's favourite weather conditions. She could sit for hours watching the rain running down the windows. The fire was on, crackling away, making music with the tap-tap-tap of the rain. She had made herself a hot chocolate and was about to sit in her favourite blue armchair to read the letter.

Almost wishing she hadn't agreed to read it, she opened the letter from Tony. Feeling nervous, she felt her heartbeat increase a notch. Why was she feeling like this? Agreeing to read the letter first had been said in haste, as she was struggling with the guilt she was managing. Knowing that she was in touch with Sally.

At first, it was nice to have Moira back in the village; she felt good helping her settle back in and taking her where she needed to go. But the more she was in touch with Sally, the less she wanted to be around Moira. She had been glad when Moira bought the car and learned to drive.

"Okay, Patsy, come on, read the letter," she chastised herself out loud.

Unfolding the single page, she noticed the handwriting was neat. She wasn't sure what she had been expecting, possibly a few scrawled lines, maybe. As she reached the end of the page, she felt a silent tear fall down her cheek.

"Oh my God, why am I feeling sorry for that animal?" she shouted out loud at the fire.

Almost throwing the letter in the fire at the same time. It was a proper and well-written apology to Moira. Tony had not been in his right mind and could no longer live with himself. Patsy wondered why he had not just handed himself in to the police.

Patsy was not sure this letter would help Moira; she knew Moira was a sensitive soul, and if the letter brought her to tears, she worried it would do Moira more harm than good. Popping a couple of logs on the fire, she listened to them crackle as the flames started to consume them. She thought about her own daughter, who was still stuck over in Ireland with Moira's husband. Patsy hated what she had done to Moira, but she loved her daughter.

Sally was very unhappy. She was pregnant and coping with a toddler that wasn't hers. Daniel was proving to be a bit of a handful. Brian, by the sounds of things, was out most of the time working, and his evenings were spent down at the local pub. By the time he came home, Daniel was asleep, and Sally was exhausted. He didn't help at all.

Sally had tried to reason with him about letting Moira see Daniel or even having shared custody with him. Brian was having none of it. He didn't want to chance taking him back to Scotland in case Moira took him back permanently. He knew she had the means to fight for full-time custody of him.

All Patsy felt she could do was encourage her daughter; more than anything, she wished Sally would choose to come home. She knew from the phone calls that things were getting tense and that they were not doing well financially. Deciding she was not going to help them with any money. Patsy felt strongly that Sally had made her bed and should lie in it. She had, however, told Sally that she would pay to get her and the children home without Brian.

Patsy had been delighted when Sally told her that she had no intention of marrying Brian. The initial attraction had long since worn off, and she sincerely regretted what had happened between them. Being pregnant was a mistake she could do nothing about.

Sighing deeply at the impossible situation and being caught between the devil and the deep blue sea with Moira and Sally, she thought sadly about how she could remedy this huge wrong.

Sitting by the fire, listening to the logs crackle and the rain tap-tapping on the window, she silently prayed that her daughter would come home. She was worried about her. She felt Sally wasn't safe over there with him.

Patsy asked herself, was it time to tell Moira any of this? She quickly decided, No, definitely not. The timing never seemed right, though. She so desperately wanted to share with Moira that she was in touch with Sally and that she knew where Daniel was. The guilt continued to gnaw away at her.

The dog barked loudly, making her jump out of her skin. The postman had let himself in the gate. Rising to meet the postman, exchanging pleasantries with him, she dumped the soggy parcel onto the kitchen table, then made herself a cold drink. Her aunt in Cornwall, whom she had met only three times in her lifetime, sent her a knitted jumper every year for winter. Every year, it went into the Christmas jumble sale at church. They were always completely unwearable and hideous.

Unwrapping the parcel and reading the card, she held up the jumper. She laughed at how awful the pattern was. It made her think about how faithful her aunt was in making the jumper she sent every year. She realised she would miss the jumpers coming when they inevitably stopped. Sipping her drink, she knew that she wanted to tell Moira about what was going on with Sally. Finding the right time was going to be hard. Moira was still in a very tender place with everything.

Patsy had never shared the attack on Moira with Sally; for some reason, it didn't feel right. She wondered if that might have made a difference; they might have come back. So many mixed feelings were crashing around in her heart. Now she had to explain her thoughts to Moira about the letter from Tony.

TWENTY-SIX

MRS A. MARSHALL

A week had passed by very quickly, too quickly in Moira's opinion. It was the day of her appointment to read the letter from Tony with Marieann.

Sitting across the table from Marieann, Moira felt a stab of deep anxiety poking at her ribs. Knowing, though, that it was time to read Tony's letter, she needed closure to move on. Marieann watched as Moira slid the letter out of its envelope. Noticing the slight tremor in her young hands as she began to unfold the sheet of paper. She noted as Moira started to read the neatly written words, that Moira's eyebrows had shot up, and her nose wrinkled a couple of times. There would be much to talk about.

Folding the letter back up and putting it back in the envelope, Moira looked at Marieann. Her eyes were full of pain and sadness. She burst into tears. It was like a floodgate had opened, releasing a torrent of pent-up emotion.

Waiting silently for the tears to slow, Marieann tentatively asked Moira what she thought of the letter.

"I'm not sure, he obviously had a tough time, but that surely does not send him to do what he did to me? I appreciate the sincerity of his apology, but I know I would have preferred him to face justice instead of taking his own life. He could have easily handed himself in."

Marieann gently took Moira's hand and told her how brave she was to have read the letter.

"You will be glad you read the letter; throwing it away would have brought more uncertainty into your mind. You have enough of that, young lady," Marieann smiled.

"It is possible he thought he was shielding you from having to relive it all with a trial?" Marieann offered.

"I don't know what he was thinking, but the letter has ended the fear of it happening again. It has also helped me to see that it wasn't my fault. I always thought I had done something to make him do that to me."

Moira blew her nose into a hanky.

"Let's do some of those breathing exercises that I have been teaching you, let's do them together," Marieann breathed in deeply, nodding to Moira to follow suit.

They chatted for the rest of the session. Leaving the hospital, Moira was glad to know that Tony could never harm anyone again. Sticking her two fingers up to the sky, she headed into the car park to find Belle.

She drove home with a mind full of mixed thoughts. Parking Belle up at the side of her house, she decided to walk up into the woods. So many times she had walked this path, with friends, with her dad, with her unborn baby. Today, she walked with her thoughts.

The path held many of her great memories and secrets. It made her wonder how many other people's secrets it held. Autumn was her favourite season of the year. The colours of the leaves and the crunch of them underfoot. The stunning skies, especially here, were breathtaking. Breathing in the fresh air, she took a moment to acknowledge all that was good.

As she walked, she allowed herself to enjoy the sights and sounds around her. It may be time to move on and look for a job. She didn't need to work; she was a wealthy woman and owned her house. She had thoroughly enjoyed her little job in Leeds and often thought about everyone she had worked with.

Tomorrow was the meeting in Glasgow with the mystery Mrs A Marshall. Her curiosity was at a peak. The office had given her no more information about the meeting, except to say that it would be in her best interests to attend. It felt all very cloak-and-dagger.

She had braved so much over the past few years; surely a meeting with a mystery person wasn't going to be the straw that broke the camel's back? Dusk was beginning to turn into darkness, and as she made her way back down the hill, she knew that tomorrow would be interesting.

After eating a hearty plate of stew, Moira made her way to the living room with a whisky and lemonade. The letter from the mystery woman was on the side table; no matter how many times she looked at it, she found no clues about what it might mean.

"So annoying," she grumbled as she popped the letter into her bag.

So much had happened to her in the last few years, she had lost two children, a husband, a best friend, she had no parents alive and had suffered a horrific attack that had left her with inward scars and outward scars.

The sessions with Marieann were fantastic; she was feeling much stronger in herself. Moving forward was the answer. Finishing the bottle of whisky, she turned in for the night. Tomorrow was a new day. She had managed today just fine. Lying her weary head on the pillow, she wondered what tomorrow would bring with the meeting at the solicitors.

Arriving at the solicitors' with about ten minutes to spare, her heart was beating fast in her chest. Moira stopped for a moment to catch her breath. She had rushed all the way up Sauchiehall Street, worried she might be late. Putting all of Marieann's breathing exercises into play for a couple of minutes gave her time to settle her mind for whatever was to come.

The building was huge, housing several businesses. An ornate stairway led up to the second floor. The hallway had a deep blue carpet that had seen many shoes. The office door was slightly ajar. Pushing it open, Moira walked into a plush space. Beautifully wallpapered with a deep, patterned, red carpet. The young girl at reception looked up and smiled.

"You must be Miss Kirkwell. Please take a seat over there. Mr Cassidy will be with you shortly."

Moira was ushered over to three large upholstered chairs with gorgeous light-blue cushions. She felt very grand sitting in their posh seats. Looking out at the bustling city below, she was interrupted by a man's voice.

"Miss Kirkwell, would you follow me, please?"

Looking up, she was met by a very handsome young man in a dark brown suit with a deep green tie. Her heart was almost bursting out of her chest with apprehension. Why had she decided to go on her own? Too late to think about that now!

Obediently following Mr Handsome, she walked into a room where four tub chairs surrounded a dark-brown oval coffee table. Sitting in two of the chairs was an older man in a grey suit with a moustache and a thin mouth. The other chair held the mystery woman. A woman slightly older than she was, with similar dark curly hair. She was dressed impeccably, making Moira feel a little underdressed for the occasion.

"Please, Miss Kirkwell, take a seat," said the older man, gesturing towards the chair opposite the mystery woman.

He reached out his hand and shook hers as he introduced himself as James Cassidy, the owner of the firm and his son, James junior, who had seated himself in the last remaining chair.

Moira looked at the woman; she seemed as nervous as Moira was feeling.

"Miss Kirkwell, I'm sure you are wondering what you are here for today? Let me introduce you to our client, Miss Angela Marshall. Miss Marshall has some news that I'm sure you will be interested in hearing. We are here to witness this exchange between you and to be of any further help in the situation for you both should you need it."

Stuttering a bit, feeling slightly overwhelmed, Moira said, "Please call me Moira."

Moira's heartbeat went up a gear. What had she done to this lady? Her thoughts were racing along at breakneck speeds.

"Moira, I'm sure you must be at your wits' end, wondering what's going on here? I won't keep you in suspense."

Her voice was low and her tone educated. Her accent was not from Glasgow; she sounded more like Moira did, from the Dumfries area.

"I believe I may be your half-sister," Angela stated.

The words hit Moira like a punch in the gut. She looked at the two men for some connection. Both just nodded towards Angela.

Angela continued to speak.

"My mother sadly died a few months ago. On her deathbed, she told me all about you. We owned the estates that surround Glendoon. My mother was in a miserable marriage and had an affair with a stableman who worked on the estate. She already had me and my older brother, Stuart. She became pregnant again while my father was away in America on business for a year. Hiding the pregnancy from everyone. She had the baby in the stables."

Angela stopped to take a breath. The following words out of her mouth surprised Moira, but she had already read Heather's letter.

"This may be hard to hear, but the stable man was your father."

Moira's head was spinning. Even though it wasn't exactly news, she still felt rocked to have the whole truth finally.

"Did my mum know about all of this?" I know she worked at the big house while my dad was the stableman. Moira felt hot tears begin to form.

"I don't know. My mum told me that your dad helped her have the baby, then took the baby home. He had told her that he and Joy were unable to have a child. I'm guessing he passed you off as a foundling."

"Why all of this mystery meeting? Could you not have just come to see me?" Moira asked in a shaky voice.

Inside, she felt that she might be on the edge of hysteria.

"Well, it's not quite as simple as that. You see, my grandmother put money from the estate into a trust fund for you to receive as an adult or if you were left on your own. I believe you received it some time back?" said Angela.

"Yes, I only found out I was not my parents' child at that time. I never knew a thing until then. I have been trying to find out what I can, but I have had other things to deal with. I'm still not sure why we are all here?"

While Moira continued to look at Angela for an answer, James began to speak.

"Angela's brother, Stuart, is contesting the trust that you received." he said.

Moira asked quietly, "How can he do that if it was all done legally?"

James answered, "We don't believe that he has any chance of winning the contest of the trust given to you. But Angela thought it might be helpful for you to know your background, and she also wanted to meet you. We felt it was the best way to go about it."

Looking around the room, Moira felt the whole thing was a little surreal. She had desperately wanted to know who she was, but now she was thinking it might be better not to know. Her head was in a whirl. Was she in any danger from this half-brother, Stuart?

Moira and Angela looked at each other Angela asked if they could have some time alone. The door closed with a soft click as the two men left the room. Moira didn't know what to say. Angela was looking at her intently. Breaking the silence, Moira asked Angela if she had any photos of her mum with her.

Pulling a few photos out of her bag, she handed them to Moira. She could see straight away where her long dark curls came from. She had this woman's nose, too. A tear began to form in the corner of her eye as she remembered how her dad had always loved her long, dark, curly hair. Was he thinking about this woman when he admired her hair?

"What was her name?" Moira asked, still looking at the photos.

"Her name was Margaret," Angela said.

Staring intently at the photos, one by one. Moira had a slew of questions, but most were for her own mum and dad and could never be answered.

"Do you know if she ever saw me again?" Moira looked up hopefully.

"Yes, she saw you a couple of times as a child in the woods. Apparently, she would walk over near where you lived to catch a glimpse of you. She attended your wedding, too."

Watching Moira taking in her mum in the photos, Angela felt quite sorry for her.

"What, she came to my wedding?"

Scanning the many faces that she could remember in her mind from her wedding day, Moira couldn't place this woman.

"Angela, what about your Father, what did he make of it all? Did he know anything?" Moira asked. The questions were filling her mind now.

"I have no idea, he died two years after he came home from America, Mum never remarried, she I believe she might have loved your dad till the day she died," Angela smiled at Moira.

"This is so much for you take in, Moira, are you ok?" Angela asked.

"It is a bit upsetting, my dad was not happy in his marriage, I'm so sad that they could never be together." Moira began to cry, thinking about how much her dad had missed out on. He had stayed with Joy for her, and she began to wonder whether they had secretly seen each other after her mum died.

Had they continued their affair all through the years she was growing up? Moira had a multitude of questions to think through.

Angela moved over to sit closer to Moira and put her hand on Moira's arm.

She asked Moira if she would like to stay in touch, "We are half-sisters after all."

"What about your brother? I don't really care about the money, Angela. He can have it."

Moira felt a sliver of worry; she didn't need the threat of another angry man.

"Don't worry about Stuart, he is an angry and bitter man, caught up in a lowlife lifestyle. His assets are frozen until he sorts out his drug problem. He doesn't have the means to find you or the brains for that matter," Angela let out a little giggle.

Covering Angela's hand with hers, Moira felt a bit of comfort knowing the truth. "Yes, I would like to stay in touch, Angela."

They continued to chat, and Moira shared a few details of her past few years.

"I wish I had never told Stuart about you now."

Angela had been horrified to hear about the terrible things Moira had endured.

"I am so glad you had that bit of money to help you move on a bit and come home," Angela smiled.

Taking a small card out of her bag, Angela said, "This is where I work, and my number is there too. Get in touch anytime, Moira. It has been lovely to meet you. I hope we meet again soon."

"Can I keep a photo of your mum?"

Moira wanted to have one to look at. It was going to take time to process this new development.

"Of course, you can have them all, Moira. We have plenty of photos. If you have any more questions, once you have processed everything, please do phone me. We can have lunch somewhere nicer than here."

With that, Angela got up, pressing a hand on Moira's shoulder, she said, "Goodbye, Moira, I am thrilled that we have met."

TWENTY-SEVEN

MOVING FORWARD

A whole year had gone by in a blur. It was March nineteen seventy-six. Moira was about to turn twenty-six. She had a good job in Dumfries as the secretary at St Joseph's College. She worked four afternoons a week, taking over from Mrs Priestly, who had been there forever, but could only work part-time now.

It suited Moira; she wasn't looking for full-time work; she just wanted to be out meeting people again. She had made friends with some of the staff and was enjoying going on the odd date with one of the younger teachers, Mr Sutton, or David, as she was allowed to call him, out of the pupils' earshot.

Starting a relationship was not something she had planned. But David had persisted in asking her out until she caved in and agreed to have lunch with him.

It had been a tough decision to start a romance after everything she had been through. Deciding to be honest from the start was easy. But telling David the things she had endured was a difficult evening; he had been so understanding and kind.

Moira had kept Helen's birth and death to herself for now.

David was a happy, solid soul. He was tall with floppy blonde hair and a ready smile. His reaction to all she had spoken to him about was to say that it was in the past, and that he only knew and cared deeply for the Moira sitting across from him now. He said he would do his very best to help her navigate any difficult days she might have.

It was early days, and taking it very slowly was going to be key.

Moira liked the way that David made her feel. He was also an only child and lived with his dad. His mum had left when he was young; he had no idea where she was or even if she was still alive. Moira's feelings towards David were growing each time they met, whether that was for lunch together, dinner or just a walk around the countryside.

Marieann was pleased to hear that Moira was dating. Her sessions were still going, but only once a month now.

Moira's relationship with Fiona was growing stronger; they got on so well, it was probably because they shared the same grief over Helen that they had formed such a strong connection. She didn't see Patsy as much; in fact, she couldn't really remember the last time they had spoken in depth or spent time together. Both women were living busy lives.

Getting in from work, Moira hung her coat up in the hall. David had been up at the weekend and fitted a row of hooks for coats in the hallway. There was a little pink card on the mat. Picking it up, she recognised Patsy's handwriting. The note let her know she would be calling to visit her around seven o'clock that evening. She was glad they would have some time to catch up. It had been a while.

She fancied some macaroni and cheese for her tea. Right on seven o'clock, the doorbell rang. Opening the door, she was happy to see Patsy with a bottle of wine in hand. The fire was on, and the front room was warm and bright. She had been working on changing the house little by little. She had bought two new large sofas.

Patsy looked around and said, "You have made the house look so nice and modern too, Moira. I love what you have done."

"Thanks, come through and let's catch up, it seems so long since we had a good chat."

After all the small talk and pleasantries were over, Moira could see that Patsy was looking a bit uncomfortable.

"Patsy, are you ok?"

"Moira, I have some news for you that you are not going to like."

"What is it?"

Moira felt her heartbeat quicken; she could sense that bad news was coming.

"Sally is coming home, she is bringing her daughter and Daniel home too, she has a few things to sort out, then we will be going over to Ireland to bring them home."

Patsy looked at Moira, waiting for her response to this latest bombshell.

"What do you mean, she's coming home? How long have you been in touch with her, Patsy?" Moira asked sharply.

Patsy began to explain all that had been going on for the past year or so. Moira's eyes widened as Patsy shared what Sally had been going through; they were having to leave Brian in secret, as he had become increasingly violent towards Sally and the children. They were not safe over there.

"Are you joking? I can't believe what I'm hearing. How long have you been in touch with her for?"

Moira felt a mix of anger and concern, anger at Patsy and concern for her son.

Patsy explained that she had to keep everything a secret because Brian had no idea that Sally was in touch with her mum.

"I was afraid you might do something and make the situation worse if you knew where he was. It has been a highly volatile few months; I had to protect Sally; she's my only child Moira."

"Patsy, you have known where Daniel has been for all this time, but left me in the dark?"

Moira was more than angry.

"Yes, but we have been making plans to bring him home; it won't be long now. Moira and Daniel will be back at home with you."

Patsy could see that Moira was agitated.

Moira's head was spinning. How on earth could Patsy have kept this to herself all this time? Furious, she stood up and told Patsy to leave.

"Moira, please, I need to tell you more."

"No, how dare you keep my son away from me? I don't actually care what Sally is going through; she shouldn't have taken him in the first place, and that's probably why it is all going horribly wrong for her. Did you really think I would want to listen to any more of Sally's sob story? Get out of my house now!" Moira shouted.

Standing up, Patsy tried reaching out to Moira, but Moira slapped her hand away, shouting again, "Get out, Patsy!"

Rushing down Moira's path in the dark, Patsy stumbled and fell onto the grass. Moira watched as she scrambled back up and made her way out of the garden onto the path to the village.

Moira thought to herself, How could she sit there and share all of that information without thinking I wasn't going to react. Grabbing the wine bottle, she poured as much as she could into her glass. Moira wished her dad were here. She wanted so much to run into his arms and feel protected from this horrible world.

Pacing up and down the living room, the thought of seeing Daniel again was giving her happy butterflies, but the idea of seeing the person who had deeply betrayed her again was making her even angrier. She could one day reconcile the thought that Patsy had been in touch with her daughter, but she knew the betrayal from Sally could never be fixed.

Pouring the last of the wine into her glass, she picked up the phone and called David. Letting go of a flood of tears, she sobbed out the events of the evening.

"Hold on, Moira, I'm coming over," he said, feeling concerned for her.

"Yes, please come over. I need you."

Moira didn't want to face these revelations alone. It would be nice to have him here.

Ten minutes later, David was at the door. Moira fell into him as he came into the house. She was distraught, and he wasn't sure what to do. Moving her into the living room, he noted the empty wine bottle and asked her if she wanted a coffee and something to eat.

Settled together on the couch twenty minutes later, they both had a hot chocolate and a cheese sandwich. How romantic, she smiled to herself. David's eyes were full of concern for her.

Not really knowing what to do, David knew he needed to ask Moira the tough questions. They had been talking about everything and anything else since he had made the coffee and sandwich.

"Moira, how do you feel about Daniel coming home?"

David looked directly at Moira as he asked the question. He was aware it was a massive thing for Moira to think about.

"I don't know, it has been so long, I thought I would never see him again. How is he going to cope? He won't know me," Moira sniffed.

Moira was still on the wobbly side of the wine, but the situation was starting to sink in. How would they all cope? She knew that there was no way she was staying in the same small village as Sally. Daniel would want to see her; she was the only 'mum' he had known. He was almost three years old.

"Oh God, David, what a mess this is. I can't think straight."

Silent tears began to fall down her face. David moved over beside her on the couch and took her into his arms. She sobbed quietly, inhaling the fresh scent of his aftershave. He smelled so good, he was so handsome; she knew she was happy to have him here.

Lifting her head, she looked up at him for a moment; he had such beautiful, eyes. Her heart skipped a beat as he leaned down to kiss her softly. Returning the kiss, Moira felt things she hadn't felt for years.

"David, would you stay the night with me?" Moira said quietly.

"Are you sure, Moira?" David asked.

"Yes, I'm sure."

Leading him upstairs, Moira closed the bedroom door with a soft click.

Surprised at herself, she had often thought about how things would be the first time she ventured into a sexual relationship, after what had happened to her; she wondered if she would ever be able to let herself be with a man again.

A ray of spring sunlight was pouring in through a gap in the curtains, lighting up David's face as he slept beside her. Last night had been wonderful; she had felt so many feelings that she never thought she would experience again. She was thankful for this gentle soul, allowing her to enjoy something she thought could never feel the same for her. In fact, it had felt better than it ever had with Brian.

Quietly, leaving him sleeping, she slipped downstairs to make some breakfast. It felt nice to get up on a Saturday morning with someone else in the house. The smell of frying bacon and the radio playing downstairs woke David up. He hadn't thought their relationship would have taken this turn so quickly. He loved Moira; he admired her strength. Now he was about to find out if she could cook!

Springing out of the bed and into the shower, he washed and dressed quickly. Popping his head round the kitchen door, he shouted above the radio.

"Good morning, Moira."

Moving towards him, she held him tightly, whispering thank you into his ear.

After they had eaten, they sat out on the back step in the bright rays of sunshine. Coffee in hand and smiling at each other, Moira broke the silence.

"What would you like to do today? Shall we go out?"

"I need to go home and get a change of clothes, more suited to going out," he said, pointing out his suit and shoes from the night before.

Half an hour later, she waved him off. Locking the doors, she headed upstairs to get herself ready. They had decided to go for a hike to the waterfalls with a sandwich and a flask of coffee. Brushing her hair through and putting it up into a ponytail, Moira heard the doorbell ring. *"That was quick,"* she thought. Bouncing down the stairs, she opened the door with a broad smile. Patsy was on the doorstep, in tears.

Twenty-Eight

Things Hit the Fan

"No, Patsy, I do not want to talk about this yet. I don't have my head around any of it. I am so angry at you, too. Please give me some space to think things through."

Moira was annoyed at her turning up. It felt so inconsiderate.

"Moira, please listen, Brian has badly beaten Sally, and she is in the hospital. I don't know yet where the children are. Brian has never known that we have been in contact. I am flying over to Dublin today. I just wanted to tell you before I went. I have the address where they live. She won't be going back to him. We will try our best to get the children," Patsy said everything in a rush.

Watching Patsy head back down the path to her car, Moira's thoughts were in turmoil. What was going to happen with all of this? Her son was in danger. She had no way of helping him. Would Patsy really try to get him or only her own granddaughter?

"Hold on, Patsy, I want to come with you," Moira shouted down the path.

"Moira, do you think that is wise?" Patsy asked as she made her way back up the path.

"Please wait for me, I am so desperate to see Daniel."

There was no way she was not going with Patsy.

Rushing back upstairs, she threw a couple of things into a bag, grabbed her passport from the top drawer and her handbag from the front room, then locked up. She dashed down the path and got into the car with Patsy.

On the drive to Glasgow, Moira started to have second thoughts about her impulsive decision. Poor David, he would be wondering where she was. She would have to call him from the airport and let him know what was going on. Daniel was her priority; even the thought of seeing him again had her heart racing. He wouldn't remember her; he had only been six months old when they had snatched him, but she remembered everything about him: his smell, the shape of his face, his tiny arms and legs. She had to grab this opportunity to get him back.

She still had the sheet from the cot that had his smell on it.

Their flight was at four o'clock. Moira was feeling nervous now, as they drew closer to the airport. She had never been on a plane before. Walking through the terminal was a strange experience; it was all so big and noisy. They had no big luggage to book in, thankfully. Making their way to the departure lounge, Patsy asked Moira how she was feeling.

Moira held back tears as she spoke, "I don't really know, I feel scared about flying, worried about my son's safety and upset that he probably won't even remember me,"

Waiting in the departure lounge with a hot coffee, Moira sought out a phone booth to call David. She felt annoyance when his dad answered, she hastily explained that she had to fly to Dublin urgently. Moira asked David's dad to say it was concerning Daniel.

She had no idea how much of her life David had shared with his dad, but she hoped he would understand why she had impulsively decided to go with Patsy.

Waiting to board the plane, Moira tried to picture her son. It was breaking her heart; she had tried so hard to work through all the feelings of loss that bombarded her every day. Now, as they sat onboard their plane, every sense was exaggerated in her heart and her mind. She was awash with questions about what he might look like and whether he would have an Irish accent. What would his reaction to her be, and how would she feel seeing Sally?

They hadn't spoken much on the drive or in the airport; it had been an awkward silence, broken by the odd piece of small talk. Once they were in the air, Patsy asked her how she was feeling about everything. She wasn't sure Patsy would like the truth, but she smiled and said she was grateful that she had told her Daniel was in danger.

Landing in Dublin was a scarier experience than taking off in Glasgow. She thought they were going to bounce back up off the tarmac with all the wind and rain. What a horrible introduction to Ireland. She had seen pictures of lush green fields, rolling mountains bathed in sunlight. But here they were in a grey city in the pouring rain. Trying not to get soaked, they ran across the tarmac to the arrivals lounge.

"We need to find a taxi to take us to St James ' Hospital. That's where Sally is. Are you sure you want to come with me?"

Patsy wasn't sure that Sally would want to see Moira. She hadn't told Sally that Moira was with her.

"I can give you the address where they have been staying if you want to see if you can find Daniel," Patsy asked.

"No, I think it would be best if we go to the house together, especially if he has hurt Sally. Surely the police will be involved?"

Moira was surprised at Patsy suggesting that she go to the house to confront Brian on her own.

Eventually, they were next up in the queue for a taxi. The Taxi took twenty minutes to get to the hospital. Patsy had the ward number written on a piece of paper. They had to go to the main reception to ask for directions. It was a busy ward. It was just after teatime. Some patients were walking around, and some were still in their beds. The matron came to speak to them before they could see Sally.

"I'm afraid you may be pretty shocked when you see your daughter. It is mainly bruising; nothing has been broken."

Motioning to them to follow her, she led them to a little side room.

Sally was propped up in bed. She turned her head to see them coming into the room.

Moira was shocked to see what Brian had done to her. Her face was a mess, her jaw was black and blue, and both her eyes were the same, swollen, black and almost shut.

Seeing her mum sent Sally into floods of tears. Moira decided to step back out of the room and let them reunite. It would be too much for Sally to face her as well.

Pouring herself a strong cup of coffee from the trolley, she sat out in the corridor to wait. She let the nurses know where she was.

Sitting there, she could only be thankful that she hadn't seen or experienced that side of Brian; he had, of course, been grumpy and had shouted at her a couple of times, but she put it down to the stress of getting married, moving and the new baby. Or maybe it was signs of things to come. The way he had treated her when he was caught out made her think.

Would it have been her lying there, had he not taken off with Sally? Lost in her thoughts, she jumped when the nurse tapped her shoulder to say she could go in to see Sally. She wondered what the nurse would think if she knew the circumstances that had brought her here.

Following the nurse into the room, she saw that Sally was sitting in a big chair beside the bed and Patsy was holding her hand. She felt a pang of jealousy almost for their relationship; they had always been close. Patsy had Sally when she was seventeen.

Apparently, it had been all the talk of the village; nobody knew who her dad was. Sally had been three years old when Patsy had married a local man. Moira hadn't really seen much of him over the years; he was always away on business.

Sally's eyes filled with tears as soon as she saw Moira.

"I'm so sorry, Moira," she kept repeating over and over through tears.

Not knowing what to do or say, she walked over and hugged her.

Even though Sally had been a part of ruining her life, she still knew how she must be feeling, sitting there in pain and probably fear. Sally had been her best friend for almost all of her life, too, and she had missed their friendship. She knew though, that they would never be friends again.

Standing up, she saw that Patsy had left the room. Now, she felt awkward, not knowing what to say.

"Why, Sally, why did you do what you did to me? You took my son; surely it was enough to take my husband, but not my son!"

Even though Sally was in a mess, Moira felt she needed answers.

Looking at her through the tears, Sally told her that she had no intention of taking her son. Everything had happened in a blur; yes, they had been having an affair, seeing each other when they could. She had no intention of taking off with either Brian or Daniel. Things had just escalated out of her control that morning. She had been shocked to see Daniel in Brian's arms when he got in the car.

She felt no comfort in her words. The bare fact was, she had taken them both.

"I want my son back, Sally. Is he safe where he is now?"

"I don't know Moira. Brian lost it completely last week. He's been getting angrier and angrier these past few months. This is not the first time he's hit me. But it's undoubtedly going to be the last. He hasn't been in to see me, and he isn't picking up the phone at the house. I have tried to call a neighbour, but they are not answering either," Sally started crying again.

"I have to get to Daniel." Moira was starting to fear for his safety.

"What you and Brian did to me almost killed me. I went out to the town one night, not long after it all, and ended up bringing a man back to the house. He almost killed me. I was in the hospital for weeks recovering. I've spent over two years in therapy. I'm fine now, but the scars are still there." Moira surprised herself, blurting out what had happened in the aftermath of them going.

"Mentally and physically, I'm never going to be the same. But I am happy now in a new relationship." Moira wanted Sally to know that she was at least happy.

Patsy returned to the room with hot drinks and sandwiches.

"We need to find the children and get them out of danger, Patsy," Moira said as soon as she came back in.

"We will, Moira, don't worry, let's leave Sally to rest and work out a plan to get to the house." Patsy wasn't sure about them going to the house on their own.

Walking through the unfamiliar hospital corridors, Moira was beginning to feel very tired. She hadn't thought about where they would be staying or about where they could eat.

"Where are we going to stay?"

Patsy reassured her that they had lodgings close to the hospital that her husband had sorted out. He would be flying in first thing in the morning.

They got another taxi to the lodgings. It was a clean, warm house. The landlady was small and thin with long black hair.

"Let me show you to your rooms, ladies, she had a lovely accent," thought Moira to herself.

Sorting out her clothes and essentials that she had thrown into her rucksack, she realised she didn't have a brush, socks or a warm jumper. She had one clean pair of trousers, a top, some knickers, and deodorant. She noticed she had no toothpaste or toothbrush either. Thankfully, at the bottom of the bag, there was a pair of blue stripey pyjamas.

Moira sat on the bed and cried. This whole situation was surreal. The night before had been such a breakthrough in helping her move forward; she felt she was now a thousand miles back. The thought of seeing Brian again was sending shivers down her spine.

She was glad they were not going to the house where the children were until morning, when Jack would be with them. Jack and Patsy had said it was best to keep the police out of it for now in case the children were taken into care; they just had to hope against hope that they were both ok.

Sitting on the bed, she watched the rain trickle down the window, lit by the streetlight, as silent tears rolled down her face.

Moira didn't know what to expect when Jack arrived. She didn't really know what he was like. Whenever he was home, Patsy always asked them to go out so he could have some space. She had often thought maybe he didn't like children around.

They had eaten their breakfast together in polite tension. Moira was desperate to get going, whereas Patsy knew they had to wait for her husband to arrive. It was just after ten when the door opened, and in he strode. He made his way into the breakfast room, hugging his wife straight away and extending a polite handshake to Moira. He nodded a greeting to her. He painstakingly had a cup of tea and some toast with marmalade. She watched him as he ate.

Jack was a tall, handsome man, a few years older than Patsy. He wore his dark hair slicked back and wore casual brown cords with a purple jumper.

Moira excused herself from the table to let them talk. Seeking out the landlady, she asked if there was a call box anywhere nearby.

"You won't be able to call over to England, I'm afraid," she said in her Irish lilt.

Disappointed, she went to her room to get her coat and put her hair up. Moira had gone down the night before to ask if there was a shop she could go to, to get the things she had forgotten. The landlady had gone into the back room, appearing a few minutes later with a new toothbrush, toothpaste, a used, clean-looking brush and a green jumper that she said she could borrow.

"People leave stuff here all the time," she said kindly.

Making her way back down to the breakfast room to see what was going on. Moira found Jack and Patsy all ready to go.

Jack had asked the landlady to book them a taxi; he had changed into brown slacks and a pale green jumper. The journey to Sally's house was pretty long, about forty minutes. They arrived in a horrible-looking, long, grubby street of back-to-back houses.

Pulling up outside number 29, Moira's heart was in her mouth.

"Maybe you should wait in the car?"

Jack said, "We don't really know what's going to happen. Brian might kick off if he sees you here, too, Moira."

The door opened from the house next door, and a young woman poked her head out and asked who they were.

"We are here to pick up the children," said Patsy.

"Who are you?, I've not seen you before," the woman peered at them suspiciously.

Patsy said, "We are Sally's parents."

"Those kids have been crying all night. I've knocked on, and he's not answering. They are still bawling up the stairs. I can hear them through my wall," she said in a broad Irish accent.

"Ok, thank you, we will try and get in," Jack said.

Jack tried the front door, but it was locked.

"Is there a back door?" Jack asked.

The neighbour led them through her house and out to the back. Jack hopped over the fence and tried the door, but it was locked too. They could hear the children crying. Jack looked at Patsy, and she nodded. He barged the door, and it didn't budge. A couple of good kicks later, the back door went in. By this time, more neighbours were gathering at the sound of the door going in.

Making his way through the kitchen with Moira and Patsy behind him, the noise the children were making was scaring Moira. Jack started to bound up the stairs, stopping dead in his tracks. He turned around and ushered Moira and Patsy back into the kitchen.

"Please wait here. I will bring the children down."

Jack gave them both a look that said, *'Don't come any further.'*

Moira and Patsy waited for the children to be brought down; there was something very wrong. They could hear the children crying even louder as they came down the stairs; the baby was screaming. Jack carried the baby and gave her to Patsy. Daniel came running out in front of him.

He was shouting "Daddy, Daddy," and pointing back at the stairs.

Moira scooped him up and tried to comfort him. He wriggled and cried. Patsy was trying to calm the baby. Both of the children were wet, upset and smelly.

"Grab the children some food, they must be starving. Ask one of the neighbours to call the police and an ambulance." Jack's face told them whatever was going on upstairs was serious.

"Stay down here with the children."

Closing the kitchen door, Jack made his way back up the stairs.

Moira was an emotional wreck; it was clear the child had no idea who she was. Her heart ached for him. What had he seen in the house? An older lady had come into the kitchen and put her arms around Moira's shoulders. She led her through the garden to her home, a couple of doors down. Let's get this little one cleaned up. Moira looked around for Patsy; she was being led away by the neighbour who had let them in through the back.

She could hear sirens approaching the street. She knew in her heart that Brian was dead. She felt nothing. He had effectively ruined her life.

"I'm Mary Kelly. I didn't know your friends well, but I often chatted to this little fella out in the garden."

Mary seemed kind. Moira had no words to say. She was in shock.

"Come on, let's get this little fella into the bath."

She brought some biscuits and a drink through to the bathroom. Daniel almost choked, shoving the biscuits into his mouth.

"Slow down, Daniel, there are plenty more. Are you very hungry?" Moira could see he was looking at her intently.

"My name is Moira, I'm your mummy's friend."

It pained her to say the words, but she knew he needed reassurance, not her blurting out something he wouldn't understand. Only God knew what he had seen in that house.

How long had they been in that room with nothing to eat? Her heart was aching for him.

The police came to the door not long after Daniel was washed and settled in a set of clothes that were a bit too big for him, but dry and clean. They had been feeding him small amounts of mash every 15 minutes. Mary had told Moira she had been a nurse; she knew that trying to give him too much at once would make him ill.

"Good afternoon, ladies, thank you so much for looking after this little man, is it Daniel? We need to take him down to the station. Considering the situation, we need to have the children placed with social services for the time being."

"Why?" Moira asked.

"Their mother is not able to look after them in hospital, and unfortunately, their daddy is dead." The young policeman didn't beat around the bush.

"Surely the children can go with their granny and grandad, isn't that better for them than social services?" Moira was struggling with the notion of losing Daniel to social services.

Moira motioned for the policeman to come into the kitchen, where she could speak to him privately.

"I am Daniel's biological mum. A couple of years ago, Sally and Brian abducted him and brought him over here. I have only just found him. Can he not go with his grandparents?"

"I'm so sorry, Miss, I can't just take your word for it. Do you have proof that he is your child?"

"You can ask Sally his so-called mother for a start, she shot back at him. Why would you take him away after what he's just been through? What good is that going to do for him?"

Moira snatched Daniel up in her arms and marched out of the house to find Patsy and Jack.

The policeman moved quickly, following her. Moira started to shout for Patsy.

Banging on the back door of the other neighbour's house, she shouted, "Patsy, Patsy, I need you, they are trying to take Daniel away."

Opening the door, Patsy was pushed aside by a frantic Moira, holding Daniel tight to her chest. The policeman rushed past her too, into the kitchen.

"What's going on?" gasped Patsy, shocked at the scene before her.

"I can't let him go again, Patsy. Please help me; the police are saying both children must go into care," Moira was almost hysterical.

"It's ok, Moira, the children do need to go into hospital to be checked over, we can go with them."

Patsy reached out to comfort Moira and little Daniel, who was now screaming for his dad and demanding to be put down.

"Please, can you explain who I am?" Moira asked.

"Of course we will, and I am sure Sally will too. We are going to have to break the news to Sally that Brian has hung himself." Patsy was concerned about telling Sally, knowing that her daughter wasn't in a good place already.

Moira allowed the policeman to take Daniel, who was still screaming. It was breaking her heart to see him in such a state.

"Moira, are you going to be ok coming to the hospital with the children, you know, Daniel will run to Sally."

Patsy moved to put her arm around Moira's shoulders.

"There is another ambulance on its way to take the children to the hospital," the policeman said.

Twenty-Nine

Going Home

Everything was going so fast. The children had been checked over and were in cots. Patsy had gone to let Sally know all that had happened. Moira was enjoying just looking at her little boy. Sally's daughter was fast asleep in the next cot. Daniel was so sweet-looking with big dark eyes and strawberry blonde hair. The cot was far too small for him; he wanted to run around.

He wasn't too severely affected physically by what he had just been through, but who knew how it had affected him mentally and emotionally. He kept asking for his mummy and his daddy. Picking him up, Moira took him to the day room, where there were a few toys for him to play with.

It was a joy for her to watch him; he played nicely with a bus that had lots of doors to open and lights that went off and on. Sitting on the floor playing with him, she thought about all that she had missed: his first steps, first words. She wondered what his first words were; would Sally remember?

"Mummy, Mummy," Daniel flew out of the open door to jump into Sally's arms.

Moira watched him with tears in her eyes. He snuggled into Sally's neck; he burst into tears and laughed at the same time. She watched Sally with him. Holding him close and telling him everything was going to be ok.

"Where's Daddy?" Daniel asked in his little Irish accent.

"Daddy's gone to live with the angel's sweetheart." Sally didn't hesitate to tell him that he wasn't going to see his daddy again.

Silent tears trickled down Moira's face as she watched the scene playing out before her. Daniel had tolerated being with her because no one else was there. She was a stranger to him.

Moira chose to stay in the day room while Sally and Patsy went to speak to the doctor about the children. She looked out the window; the frame was painted a dark green, and the glass was dirty with fingerprints. Life was going on out in the hospital grounds. Nurses with their own lives, doctors, patients and children coming and going to appointments. So many lives, were any of them facing the agony she was facing right now? She felt so alone. Who would help her with Daniel? She wasn't sure that David would be willing to take on a small child that wasn't his. She wasn't even sure in that lonely moment that she could manage the monumental task of reconnecting with her son.

Moira felt a warm hand on her shoulder catapult her out of her thoughts. She turned and looked at Jack. His face was etched with the stress of the past few hours. Jack opened his arms for Moira to come to him.

"I'm so sorry, Moira, you have so much to manage in this horrible situation. I salute your bravery for even coming over with Patsy." Jack's heart went out to this young woman; he hadn't seen much of her growing up. But he knew she had already weathered more than most.

Moira, allowing herself to really cry, sobbed, "He doesn't know me. How am I going to manage this? He can't just lose his dad and then be expected to be thrust into the lives of strangers."

"I don't know how this is going to work, Moira, but we will support you and Sally through this," Jack said, feeling deep compassion for Moira.

Moira felt a stab of grief for her parents; Sally was so lucky to have her parents. Moira was deeply aware she was on her own in life.

"I want to see how Daniel is. Are you going to the ward?" she asked Jack.

Walking into the ward, Moira watched Daniel playing with a car on Sally's knee. The baby was still fast asleep in the cot. Daniel looked at her with his big brown eyes.

Her heart flipped. "Daniel, why not show Moira your car?"

Sally tried to shove him off her lap.

"No, Mummy, I don't want to." Daniel looked up at Sally with fear in his eyes.

He had been through too much. Moira stood for a while watching this little family before she left the ward.

Following her out of the ward, Patsy called after her. "Moira, are you okay?"

"Of course I'm not bloody okay, Patsy. My husband, not Sally's, has killed himself. My son doesn't have a clue who I am, and you are asking me if I am okay!"

Moira was angry. She wished she hadn't come to Ireland at all.

"Moira, we are going to bring the children home, but they need to stay in the hospital for a few of days. The police will want to speak to Sally. We are going to stay a couple of days,"

Patsy hugged Moira.

"I'm so sorry, Moira."

Feeling defeated, and utterly exhausted by the turn of events, Moira said, "I am going back to the digs to get my things. It will be best if I go home and wait for you all to get back home."

Sighing, Moira hugged Patsy back, saying her goodbyes.

Over Patsy's shoulder, she saw Sally and Daniel at the ward door watching them. She waved at Daniel and blew him a kiss.

"Bye-bye, darling child," she said quietly.

"Please bring them home, Patsy."

Moira walked away towards the hospital entrance on her own.

Sitting on the bed in her room at the digs, Moira knew it was time for her to go home. It had been an exhausting day. Brian was dead; he had taken his own life. Daniel didn't have a clue who she was, his daddy was dead, and his 'mummy' was in hospital because of Daddy.

She had no idea how to book a flight. The landlady had told her there was a train to Larne and a ferry across to Stranraer in the morning. That seemed an easier option and would give her some precious time alone to think through the situation. She didn't want to talk to Patsy or Jack; she had heard them coming in later that night and had pretended to be asleep when she heard a light tap on the door.

Tossing and turning all night, dreaming about Daniel, worrying about how this whole mess was going to sort itself out, she got up feeling more tired than she had when she went to bed.

There was a note under the door. Opening it, she read that the children had stayed in the hospital overnight with Sally. Patsy had written that they were going back up to the hospital in the morning. She had finished the note, saying they knew she was making her way home today, but would let her know what was going on here when they could.

She rolled the note up and threw it into the bin. She looked at the bag on her bed, all ready for the trip back to Scotland. The landlady had booked her a cab to the bus station to get the coach to Larne.

Arriving at Stranraer nearly six hours later, she was exhausted. She had changed her punts back to pounds. Now she had another long bus ride from Stranraer to Dumfries. It would be dark by the time she got there. Gathering some change together, she made her way to the phone boxes to call David. He must be worried sick about her.

Again, it was his dad who picked up the phone. He wasn't home from work. His dad said he would let him know that she would be arriving in Dumfries around 7 o'clock that evening.

She had thought long and hard on the journey home. The ferry crossing had made her sick, spending half of her time in the toilets throwing up, and she vowed to fly next time if she ever revisited Ireland. She was glad to see dry land again. Settling herself into a seat on the coach, she slept a good part of the way.

She woke up and stretched. The coach wasn't busy; only a few people were still on it. The bus pulled in at one of the many stops along the route. She noticed an elderly couple getting on. The man was helping his wife, who was almost bent in two, to get up the steep steps of the coach, making sure she was settled into the nearest seat to the door before settling down himself.

Smiling to herself, she thought about David and whether they would make it to that stage in life, growing old together. It was too dark now to see anything other than the passing headlights of cars going the opposite way. Allowing herself to think about Daniel, she thought about how they would manage to transition him over to her care. Would he accept her? Would it work if they all lived in the same village? So many questions were buzzing around in her mind with no answers. She pictured her little boy in her house, running up the stairs, dashing out into the garden. His golden curls bouncing around, looking up at her, and clinging to her legs, calling *her* Mummy. What was going to be best for Daniel? How would her fledgling relationship with David manage the introduction of a lively toddler? If they went on to have children, what would that look like?

"Oh God, what a mess," she said out loud through gritted teeth.

Closing her eyes, she imagined her mum and dad in the house with her and Daniel. Knowing the stark reality of that never happening made her fill up, and she began to cry quietly; the events of the days before were catching up with her. Pulling some hankies out of her bag, she wiped her face and tried to straighten her thoughts out. She thought about the week ahead: going back to work, explaining to people where this child had suddenly appeared from. It all sounded so strange when she tried to make sense of how it would all pan out.

Now she just wanted to get home to rest and see David, the bus eventually pulled up at the Sands. Thankfully, she had enough to get a taxi home. Waiting patiently as the elderly couple made their way painfully down the stairs, she wished she had got off first to be of some help to them. Getting off the bus, her legs felt like jelly. Exhausted, she made her way across the road to call a taxi and David.

"Moira, Moira," she heard David call her name. The relief that shot through her almost caused her legs to buckle.

David bounded up to her like a happy puppy, scooping her up in his arms and holding her tightly.

"Let's get you home," David said.

Sleeping most of the way home, she felt a bit wobbly getting out of the car. Once inside, it was straight upstairs and into bed for her. David was calling the shots. Making her a hot drink, he wasn't surprised to see her fast asleep, fully clothed, on top of the bed. He folded the blankets over her and left the room. He had told the school that neither of them would be in the next day. Locking up the house and putting the chains on, he made his way to sleep in the spare room.

It was 11 am before he heard Moira moving around upstairs. Calling up to her, he let her know he was there. He didn't want to startle her coming down to someone in the house.

"David, you are here already. How did you get in?" Moira asked as she walked into the kitchen.

"I stayed the night, Moira. I slept in the spare room. You must be ravenous. When did you last eat?"

Moira wasn't sure when she had last eaten; she had brought a sandwich and a drink onto the bus and had both at some point.

David poured a large glass of water and placed it in front of Moira, who was sitting at the kitchen table.

"Drink this first, it will help," David said, watching as she downed the water.

She looked so pale; he knew he loved Moira very much and wanted to support her in any way he could.

Making scrambled eggs and toast, he asked her gently if she wanted to talk about what had happened in Ireland. Taking a big sip of her coffee, Moira began to speak.

Listening to the whole story unfold, he marvelled at this small, strong woman who was sitting opposite him. How had she managed everything she had gone through?

"Moira, how have you managed all of this?" David could hardly believe all that he was hearing.

"I have no idea, David, but what I do know is that my body is telling me it was tough."

"It is time to rest and recover from this ordeal and build up your strength for Daniel coming home," David said.

"But what would be best for Daniel?" she thought. This had been the question that had stayed at the front of her mind the whole time. Watching him cling to his 'mummy' had been soul-destroying.

She wanted to rush over and grab him back and tell him, "No, I'm your mummy."

But, how could she do that to this traumatised little boy, who knew what else he had seen in his short life with Sally and Brian, had he seen Sally being beaten by his daddy? Had Brian hurt him in any way? There was so much she knew nothing about. It was going to be a huge process. Now that she was home, she had no way of finding out what was going on in Ireland. She wished she had taken the landlady's number.

"I wonder when they will all come home, David?"

She looked out of the kitchen window, trying to picture her son playing in the garden.

THIRTY

BETRAYED AGAIN

The waiting game was over. Moira and David had been enjoying an evening of watching the telly and having a quiet drink when the phone rang. It was Patsy.

"Oh my gosh, Patsy, are you home? Is Daniel with you?" Moira asked questions quickly.

"Moira, can we come up to your house?"

"Yes, yes, of course you can."

Putting down the phone, Moira gave a little skip of excitement. Was Daniel with her? Was Patsy bringing him straight to her?

Moira's heart was lurching in her chest. Peering out into the gloom, she watched Patsy's car stop and the lights go off. Patsy and Jack got out of the car and made their way up the path.

There was no sign of Daniel. Moira's heart sank.

Ushering them into the living room and offering them a drink, which they refused, she waited to hear what they had to say.

"Come on, Patsy, I need to know if Daniel is with you?"

"Moira, we arrived home late last night, but Sally and the children have gone back to the house in Dublin."

"Why? Why are they not coming home? You promised you would bring him home," Moira burst into tears.

Jack started to explain that Sally wanted to settle the children down where they knew home to be. They had been through so much. Sally had said that it would be too much to move them straight to a new place. The baby wasn't as affected as Daniel; he had seen and heard too much and needed the stability of settling down for a week or so before making the journey back to Scotland.

"We have filled the cupboards and left her with enough money to see her through for a couple of weeks.. The rent on the house has been paid. We put in the notice to leave at the same time Moira," Patsy explained.

Jack said, "I am going over to help her travel over with the children in two weeks."

"I can't believe I have to wait another two weeks. I wish I had stayed now and just brought Daniel home with me. I'm angry that he is still not with me."

"I'm so sorry, Moira, we did try our best to get Sally to at least let us bring Daniel home. She was adamant that he needed to settle first."

Patsy felt so sorry for Moira. There was nothing they could do about it; they had to wait and trust that Jack would bring them home.

"I just want my son back, but I understand just how hard it is to deal with trauma as an adult, so it must be even harder for a child who can't express how they are feeling."

Moira felt angry and defeated.

David stood up and gently suggested to Patsy and Jack that it might be time for them to leave, as Moira had a lot to think through.

Patsy and Jack made their way down the path with heavy hearts. There was nothing they could do to improve the situation. Sally had insisted that she was not coming back with them until she had settled Daniel. Patsy had pleaded with her to change her mind.

Getting into the car, they looked at each other, not knowing what to say.

Moira watched them drive off.

"Why, David, why! I don't understand what's going on here. I am once again denied my son, through no fault of mine, just because Sally says,"

Bursting into angry tears, Moira raced up the stairs and threw herself onto her bed, burying her screams of frustration into the pillow.

Tears soaked her pillow; none of them had a clue about how this was affecting her. Of course, she got it. It didn't mean she agreed with it. Daniel should have been brought home. She should have stayed and waited to bring him home, but she hadn't, and now she was facing the consequences of her decision.

Punching the pillow, she could see herself in her dressing table mirror, red in the face, curls sticking out everywhere, and tears running down her face. *"What's next,"* she thought angrily.

David had the telly on when she eventually came down; she went straight to the kitchen to make a drink for them both. She fancied a hot chocolate. As the kettle boiled, she thought about David, caught up in the middle of all of this. Was it time to end their relationship? Did David really want to be tied to her, a toddler and all the drama that seemed to surround her?

Popping some marshmallows on the top of the hot chocolates, she reached into the biscuit tin for two orange club biscuits. Settling into the couch after presenting him with the hot chocolate, she asked him if he could put the telly off to allow them to talk.

"What do you really think of this whole drama? Am I wrong to want my son? Do you think he will settle with me? How would you manage getting to know a toddler?" Moira blurted out some of the questions that had been building up in her mind.

"Those are big questions, Moira. I don't think I'm at all qualified to answer them. The whole thing has blown my mind. Just as we had cemented our relationship, you vanished off to Dublin, and now all of this has unfolded. Of course, you're not wrong to want your son. As for whether he will settle with you, only time will answer that. As for me, would I manage a toddler in my life, I could only try my best." David replied.

"I'm so confused by it all, David."

"I think the only way to answer any of your questions is to go and get your son. It would be a risk, he will not be happy to start with, and you will have to give up your job until he goes to school."

David looked at Moira's troubled face, knowing that he genuinely didn't have the answers she was looking for.

Pointing at David, Moira exclaimed, "Another consideration, if Sally came back here to stay, Daniel would have that bond with her that I would need to acknowledge. We might need to move away."

Shaking his head, David said, "You know I can't move away; my dad needs me to look after him for now."

Disappointment shot through her. She knew he would have moved with her if his dad wasn't in the picture, but it didn't lessen the sting of disappointment that moving wouldn't be an option.

"I think I need to go and speak to Sally myself, without Patsy and Jack. I need to get some clarity on this," Moira said quietly.

Heading up to bed later that night, a plan was forming in her mind. There had to be a way to work this out in everyone's best interests. She was going back to Dublin and this time flying there and back. Not a chance she was doing the long ferry journey again.

Moira had given herself time to calm down and think things through clearly. The flight to Dublin had been booked. She wasn't announcing her visit; she felt it best to arrive unannounced. Her anger towards Sally had subsided enough that she believed she could have a rational conversation about Daniel.

She thought about how troubled she had been when she found out she wasn't who she thought she was. The drive in her to keep Daniel from finding out his truth in later life was making her to do something about it now.

She had to think about Daniel's well-being. What if Sally couldn't cope? Whose child would she give up first? The thought of that happening made her even more determined to strike a deal with Sally to parent her son.

Even though Daniel was clearly attached to Sally, Moira knew that her son had to come home with her.

The flight was uneventful. Making her way through the airport, she rummaged in her bag for the address of the house. There were plenty taxis waiting at the airport taxi rank. She got into one and gave the address. Her heart was beating fast. She felt a stab of fear about the outcome of her visit. David had volunteered to come with her, but she knew that would be a distraction. Moira felt sure she could make Sally see sense on her own.

Pulling up outside the house, she noticed the front room curtains were closed. Surely they were up and about; her heart leapt at the thought of what they had found the last time they were here. She cocked her ear to see if she could hear the children. Maybe they had gone out.

She knocked loudly on the door.

Nothing.

She knocked again. Lifting the letterbox, she called in, "Hello, Sally, it's Moira."

She couldn't see or hear anything through the letterbox. Assuming they were out, she put her bag on the doorstep and sat on it, intending to wait for them to come home. She hoped they hadn't gone far.

Moira could see curtains twitching across the street. She wondered if anyone remembered her from the last time she was here.

After sitting patiently on the cold, hard step for half an hour, it was clear this was not going to work in the long term. Moira had noticed a couple of curtains twitching, looking to see who was there on Sally's doorstep. She didn't care; if anyone asked, she would tell them exactly why she was sitting there.

Deciding enough was enough, Moira got up and knocked on the neighbour's door, hoping they would remember her. Thankfully, they did.

"Hi, I'm visiting Sally and the children. Do you know if they will be back soon?" Moira asked.

"Oh my dear, you must come away in. Sally and the children moved out last week."

The neighbour looked at Moira with concern as she leaned on the wall. Moira had gone deathly white.

"Are you okay there? Did you not know they had gone home to Scotland?"

The neighbour's words made no sense.

Moira allowed herself to be led into the living room. She sat down hard on the couch, not knowing what to do next.

"They never came home to Scotland, that's why I'm here for my son Daniel," Moira said with tears filling her eyes.

How could she? Moira could not believe that Sally had done a runner with the children. The neighbour told Moira they had taken off the day after Patsy had left, which meant that Sally had no intention of coming home or bringing Daniel back to her.

Moira had something to eat and hot coffee before leaving in a taxi for the airport. She had thanked the neighbour for everything. She knew now that she had no choice but to go to the police and report Daniel as a missing person again. She believed she may never see him again.

THIRTY-ONE

SADNESS

A sadness swept over her as she sat in her kitchen looking out at the trees in the garden. What had she done to deserve such misery in her life? From being given away to her dad after she was born, to now, sitting here facing the fact that her son could be lost to her forever.

What would have happened to her had Margaret's husband been at home, and she had been passed off as his? She might have been brought up in a big house with a sister and a brother. She thought about the many lonely nights and long winter days when she had been yearning to have siblings to play with, to fight with and giggle with under the covers at night.

Any wonder her mother had been so miserable all the time, bringing up someone else's child? Her mum still had to live with the bitter pill of infertility and infidelity. As for her dad, why had he not told her, even when her mum had died, he could have said it then. Maybe they thought it was best that she knew nothing until they were gone. But, had he not died she would have found out anyway. Maybe he thought she would understand being twenty-one.

There she was in the woods, hiding her shame of having a child so young, all the time they were covering up someone else's same shame! There was an anger growling around in her soul. She had gone to the Gardai in Ireland and to the police here in Dumfries, reporting Daniel as a missing child.

All she could do was cherish the memory of playing with him in the hospital. Neither police force seemed very interested. She felt a deep-rooted sadness for Daniel and for herself.

Moving to sit at the back door, she sipped on her second coffee of the morning. Moira wondered if her life would ever slow down. Would she ever feel normal again? She had a deep desire to pack a few things into Belle and take off into the sunset. Who would truly miss her? David could easily move on and find the love of his life. Patsy was not talking to her at all after she told her that she had reported Daniel as a missing person.

"You have made my daughter out to be a criminal," she had shouted when she told her what she had done.

Moira had called Marieann when she got back, filling her in on the current state of affairs. They had chatted for hours, grateful for Marieann's care. Moira had sent her a huge bouquet of flowers and chocolates. Even after her call with Marieann, Moira felt a deep-set sadness in her chest.

By all accounts, Sally had disappeared with the children. Moira was unaware whether anyone had attended Brian's funeral. She had loved Brian deeply before catching him with Sally. The scars from his betrayal had taken a long time to heal. Now she felt waves of grief over his death. She replayed some of their happier times, especially the courting days in Leeds.

Who was really in the wrong in all of this? Was she in the wrong? Had she not been a good wife? Was it Sally for pursuing her husband? Was it Brian for falling into Sally's arms? Maybe she had just been caught up in the romance of it all, what if Brian wasn't who she should have married?

There were no answers to all of her questions, just a load of carnage and grief left behind. A dead husband, a missing child and an ex-best friend. Her heart ached for Daniel. She had held him in her arms for months as a baby and once again as a toddler. Why? Oh, why? Had she not taken him that day? Her own feelings had got in the way. She hadn't coped well with what happened and returned to the safety of her home. She had believed that Sally and Daniel would come back with Patsy and Jack.

Taking another sip of her coffee, she realised she had been thinking more than drinking; it was cold. She had two weeks off work to help her get over everything that had happened. She had another appointment with Marieann that afternoon. Driving into Dumfries, she thought again about disappearing. It seemed so tempting. She had the money; she also had her house to come back to if she wanted to, or realised she didn't want to disappear.

Standing up and putting her coffee cup in the sink, she wiped away a tear. Would she ever feel happy again?

THIRTY-TWO

NEW BEGINNINGS

Stepping into the room, Moira smiled at Marieann, saying, "Lovely flowers you have there."

"Yes," she replied, "I got them from a very dear friend."

They embraced before taking their seats in this very familiar setting. Moira began talking. She told Marieann everything, including how deeply sad she felt.

"In fact, Marieann, I feel like running away forever, maybe I could reinvent myself, not be Moira anymore."

Marieann carefully pointed out that if she did that, how would Daniel ever find her again?

Marieann had raised one of her highly plucked eyebrows at her, "Do you really think that would solve all of your problems?"

The more Moira thought about the idea of being someone else, the more it appealed to her. She could go to multiple places and be whoever she wanted to be.

"I don't know Marieann, but I am tired of being me right now. I want to find some joy in life for a change."

As Moira got up to leave, Marieann grabbed her hand. "Moira, this too shall pass. Please don't do anything rash. You might regret it."

Walking through the corridors of Cresswell hospital, she noticed the sign for the mortuary, the phrase 'you're a long time dead' came to mind. It made her think of her mum, who had literally just keeled over one day and died.

Her heart was pounding at the thought of simply taking off. Was it excitement or fear she was feeling? She had experienced a fear that had almost killed her. She had endured enough loss and pain in her life. It was time to kick up some dust. Strangely, it was all Marieann's doing. The sessions had given her a strength on the inside over the years and plenty of coping mechanisms for when the feelings all got too much.

Belle was sitting in the bright, April sunshine, waiting for her. Driving home, she had a mind full of ideas. Stopping at a train crossing, she thought about Daniel. What if Sally brought him back? What if she missed that? What if her son thought she had deserted him? An impatient beep behind her brought her back into the moment. Her resolve to go and start a life elsewhere began to wax cold.

Stopping in the village to get some bits in for her evening meal, she saw Patsy coming out of the post office. She waved, but Patsy ignored her. It added to her lengthy list of losses. Moira had known her all of her life; she had been a tower of strength after the attack. Now their relationship was broken.

What about David? She thought about their relationship; it was nice, but was it going anywhere? Searching her heart, she couldn't truthfully say that she loved him enough to stay and settle down with him. He was kind, funny, and the sex was good. He had gently helped her over that hurdle. But, no, he wasn't enough to keep her here.

Telling David was going to be hard. There was no rush. She wanted to make a plan first. It was exciting to think about it. Thinking about it might be enough to settle her mind.

Parking Belle at the gate, she walked past her house up to the church graveyard to visit her parents grave. She didn't come very often; it felt strange to her looking at a piece of stone in the ground, knowing they were lying underneath it. Her dad probably wasn't even that happy being stuck with her mum in death. She chuckled out loud as she thought about that.

The flowers she had taken at Christmas were long dead. Plucking them out of the metal vase, she plopped them into the bin. Emptying the vase, she turned it upside down so it wouldn't fill with water. Why was she doing that? She must have seen her mum do it many times; she had been dragged to the graveyard to tend to somebody's grave with her mum. What would Joy have made of all this? Moira smiled to herself as she thought about her mum's reactions to things.

Looking up at the woods from the graveyard, she started walking towards them. She needed to go and be where she had given birth to Helen. The woods were springing into life. It was lovely seeing all the spring flowers, new leaves, and buds everywhere. It was a season of new things. Her thoughts of moving on to new pastures were reignited. Stopping close to where she had given birth to Helen, she tried to picture what she might have looked like at eleven years of age. She would have been growing into that stage of leaving childhood, heading into teenage years. An in-between age where she was neither here nor there.

In her mind, she pictured Helen skipping up the hill in a bright red dress, white ankle socks and blue shiny patent shoes. Her hair was long, red and curly, waving about as she made her way up the hill to the woods. A twig snapped behind Moira, knocking her out of her thoughts. Turning round, she saw Fiona Barnes walking towards her. Their friendship had grown strong over the years.

"You were so still there, Moira, what were you thinking about?"

"I was watching Helen coming up the hill," Moira replied sadly, Fiona asked her if she was ok.

"No, not really, so much has happened, recently," Moira said.

"Shall I walk with you? You can come in for a catch-up. I've not seen you for a while," Fiona asked.

They walked together in silence until they got to the gate of the farm.

"I remember it all so clearly," Moira spoke quietly. "I can still feel the fear of getting caught mixed in with the fear of something happening to my baby if you hadn't found her in time."

"You must have been so scared, but you did the right thing," Fiona said.

"I was in so much pain. My head was spinning. The adrenaline of it all kept me going. The thought of getting caught was terrifying. I had to go to school the next day. I will never really know how I got through the two weeks after the birth, the pain, the guilt and the fear. I was scared that you might not keep her. My heart leapt when I heard my mum declare that you had had a 'surprise' baby. Everything in me wanted to leap in the air for joy. But, I couldn't. I had to sit there as a surly teenager feigning disinterest," Moira remembered sadly.

"And then when I heard that Helen had died, I felt such a wave of grief and sadness. I thought if I had kept her, she wouldn't have died, not that I am blaming you," Moira was quick to add.

"I was angry, grief-stricken and felt so, so guilty about it all. But no one knew Helen was mine. I couldn't show any of my feelings. It was horrible. I had to come and see you that day."

Bursting into tears, Moira leaned into Fiona's arms, letting her grief spill out in waves of hot tears.

Fiona walked Moira down to the house. The fire was still burning. The warmth seemed to make Moira more emotional. Fiona instinctively knew to let her cry, shout or scream if she wanted to. She knew the pain of grief after losing her husband and her daughter.

Fiona watched as Moira sobbed at her kitchen table, she could only imagine the pain she was in. Enduring so much in such a short space of time, she was so proud of how Moira had got on with life after it all. Even though Moira was strong, Fiona could see she was also struggling with deep-rooted pain and sadness. A good release was just what she needed. It had been ten years since Alice (Helen) had died. Fiona's dream of being a mother had been short-lived. When Moira came to her to tell her she was Helen's mum, it was a shock but also a comfort. They had been able to grieve together.

When Moira lifted her head, she could see that Fiona was still sitting in her fireside chair, staring into the crackling logs.

"A penny for them, Fiona?"

Fiona smiled to herself and asked Moira quietly, "How did you imagine Helen coming up the hill? What did she look like?"

Moira described how she saw Helen coming up the hill. Fiona nodded in agreement.

Fiona shared, "Yes, I often picture her with long red hair. I wonder if she would have been clever at school; she was as bright as a button."

The two women sat in comfortable silence for a few minutes, Fiona in her fifties and Moira in her twenties, each with their own thoughts. Getting up to make a pot of tea, Fiona asked Moira what she was thinking about.

"I can see you have a head full of thoughts, what's happening in there, Moira?"

After a couple of hours, Moira had shared all the recent events, her plans to move away, and why she felt it was the right thing to do.

"You are young, my advice is, go and see the world. Experience some new places and people. Mind you, it may leave you feeling like you don't want to come back to your little village ever again."

Waving Moira off down the lane, Fiona hoped that she would take the opportunity to go and have some fun. Making her way back into the house, she closed the door and sat back in her chair, and thought about Alice/Helen and her husband Gavin.

Thirty-Three

Carpe Diem

The village had grown in the last ten years, and Moira would have no trouble renting out the house while she was away. It would make a good family home. Packing away most of her personal things into the attic had been a big job. The locksmith had just left after putting a lock on the attic door.

David knew nothing about her plans. Moira was dreading telling him; she had put it off more than once. As time went on, she knew she would have to say to him soon. They hadn't seen as much of each other in the last month as David's dad had been quite poorly. David was all he had. Most nights, he had stayed at his own house, which made what was to come seem a little more straightforward.

David's dad was almost fully recovered, so she had invited him over for dinner, and asked him to stay the night. Sitting in the bath, she was going over how she would break the news to him about her plans. She wasn't going to spoil the evening; she would tell him over breakfast. That way, he could leave for work and think it over.

Dressing carefully for the evening ahead, she thought about what a great time she had had getting to know David. In her mind for the past month, she had started to separate from him and tried not to focus on the feelings she did have for him. They just weren't strong enough to keep her here.

She was nervous; this was going to be a big adventure. She was sorry about letting David down and leaving the village again, but she knew, deep inside her soul, that she wanted to be free and fly; she wanted to be someone else. She wanted to really live. See how it panned out. And if it didn't work out, she would do it again somewhere else. If it all finally went pear-shaped, she would come home and make the best of it.

The fly in the ointment had been Daniel. What if he came home? That had bothered her greatly until Fiona volunteered to let her know. She would call Fiona once a week for two reasons: one to let her know she was alive and well, and two to find out if there was any news on Daniel.

Putting the finishing touches to her mince round and popping it in the oven with some roast potatoes around it, she heard David coming in the front door.

"Hello, it's only me," he called, closing the door behind him.

Hearing that cheery voice made her smile. He was the loveliest man. She hoped one day he would meet someone equally lovely.

They ate, they drank wine, and Moira had a couple of whiskies with lemonade. Dragging David off the couch and upstairs to bed. She knew this would be their last night together. She made it as good as she could. Curling up beside him, once they were spent, she felt a pang of guilt. Would he get over her? Would he be ok? Kissing his cheek, she turned over and slept. She was up with the larks in the morning, making David a good breakfast.

Moira watched David's face fall. She could see the pain and disappointment in his eyes as she explained what she thought she had to do.

She reassured him that she did indeed love him very much, but, considering all she had been through, she wanted him to understand that it wasn't him; it was her need to find freedom from everything that was driving her. Maybe it would work, perhaps it wouldn't, but she knew without a doubt she had to give it a try.

She had put so much work into her counselling sessions with Marieann, Moira had grown as a person and needed to put into practise all that she had learned.

"Moira, you have been a light in my life. I love you dearly. I think I know what you need to do. I can't say I am happy about it, but what would you have done if I said you had to stay?" David smiled at her as he rose from the kitchen table.

He beckoned her over to him.

David hugged her so tightly before he left for work that she thought her ribs would snap. He had assured her that he understood, even though he didn't, David told her, he was hurt and disappointed.

Whispering into her ear, he said, "I will wait for you, Moira, for a year. I love you and want to give you this freedom, but I also want you to know I will be here for you if it doesn't work out the way you thought it might."

Moira looked up at this handsome, patient man who had helped her realise that good men existed; his eyes had filled with tears.

"I hope you meet someone soon, David. Please don't wait for me."

Moira didn't want the weight of that promise around her neck; she made him say that he wouldn't wait for her.

Watching him leave the house for the last time, she felt a tiny sliver of regret. What if this wasn't the right thing to do?

Regardless, she knew she had to find out.

Sitting in his car, David wiped his eyes. Saying a silent prayer for Moira to stay safe and come back to him, he drove off. Stopping at Patsy's he told her of Moira's plans.

The phone started to ring in the living room a few minutes after she watched David drive off.

"I wonder who that is?" she asked herself.

Picking up the phone, she heard Patsy's voice asking her if she was alright.

"Yes, of course I am alright, what do you want, Patsy?" Moira snapped.

"I know you have been angry with me and I understand why, Moira, and I know I have been very angry at you over reporting Sally to the police for taking Daniel. But I wanted you to know that I love you and want us to stay in touch." Moira wondered if someone had told her she was going away.

"Patsy, I'm leaving the village today. I have to find some freedom, live my life and seek out some adventure. Things have been bleak for too long."

"I wish you well, and I do understand Moira. Please keep in touch and let me know you are okay. I promise to tell you if I hear anything from Sally."

Moira put her hand on her heart, "Thank you, Patsy. I will stay in touch with you and Fiona. I'm happy you called. I'm sorry we spent the last while not talking, but maybe it was for the best."

Putting the phone down, Moira felt a sense of peace. Looking around at the house. Indulging in some happy memories here, she knew it was time to go and make her own happy memories.

Putting her two suitcases into Belle's boot and back seat, she was all set to go. Moira was heading to London. It was a bold move. She had a live in job as an Au pair. Looking back at the house and the woods, she whispered goodbye to the village, Helen, & her parents.

It was time to seize the day.

****

Acknowledgements

Matt Bird my friend and typesetting genius. What would I do without you?

Leigh Bowman Perks - thank you for having me as part of your *Write to Inspire* cohort.

The Inspiring Leadership Foundation Publishing House for carrying my book.

Sarah McGeough for being her wonderful self.

My husband Brian and daughter Georgie, you have been so patient with me. I am all yours now.

There are too many people to name individually, so many from *Write That Book* with Michael Heppell and many from *Write to Inspire*. Actually, I will name my *Write to Inspire* buddies. Leann, Mehnaz, Nadine, Donna, Jamie, Chadia, Aleasha, and Chelle. Keep writing guys.

Family & friends for bearing with me as I droned on and on about characters, plots, places and questions like, 'Did answer phones exist in the 1970's'!

Writing a novel is hard work. No one knows except other authors how lonely and difficult it can be.

I am grateful to all my praying friends who have rallied around and helped me over the finishing line.

Will there be a part two? Yes, there will be......

ABOUT THE AUTHOR

Helen Oxenham is the pen name of Fiona Myles. Fiona was adopted as an eight-month-old baby. She had a wonderful childhood being brought up in a small Scottish village, until being told she was adopted. As a teenager she drifted into addiction & living homeless in London in the 1980's continuing in addiction for many years until she became a Christian in 1996.

Like many people covid brought a change in circumstances and her friend Tarnya suggested she start writing. Thinking writing was above her intellect she eventually gave it a try. Twelve books later, here we are with her first novel.

Fiona has written many books over different genres. From her Sparkles the Wonder Dog series of Children's books to her best-selling books Adoption Trauma and Georgie Me & ADHD.

Connect with Fiona and browse her book collection through her website: https://fionamylesauthor.com